LESA CLINE RANSOME

ONE BIG
OPEN SKY

HOLIDAY HOUSE ⋅ NEW YORK

In memory of my mother, Ernestine Lenora Cline
(March 29, 1925–May 25, 2023),
whose love was as wide as One Big Open Sky

HOLIDAY HOUSE is registered in the U.S. Patent and Trademark Office
Printed and bound in June 2025 at Sheridan, Chelsea, MI, USA.
First Paperback Edition
3 5 7 9 10 8 6 4 2
www.holidayhouse.com

Library of Congress Cataloging-in-Publication Data

Names: Cline-Ransome, Lesa, author.
Title: One big open sky / Lesa Cline-Ransome.
Description: First edition. | New York : Holiday House, 2024. | Audience:
Ages 8–12. | Audience: Grades 4–6. | Summary: "In the 1870s, a Black
family undertakes a perilous wagon journey westward for a tenuous shot
at freedom in Nebraska"—Provided by publisher.
Identifiers: LCCN 2023034373 | ISBN 9780823450169 (hardcover)
Subjects: CYAC: Novels in verse. | Wagon trains—Fiction. | Frontier and
pioneer life—Fiction. | African Americans—Fiction. | United
States—History—19th century—Fiction. | LCGFT: Novels in verse.
Western fiction. | Historical fiction.
Classification: LCC PZ7.5.C56 On 2024 | DDC [Fic]—dc23
LC record available at https://lccn.loc.gov/2023034373

ISBN: 978-0-8234-5016-9 (hardcover)
ISBN: 978-0-8234-6062-5 (paperback)

EU Authorized Representative: HackettFlynn Ltd, 36 Cloch Choirneal,
Balrothery, Co. Dublin, K32 C942, Ireland. EU@walkerpublishinggroup.com

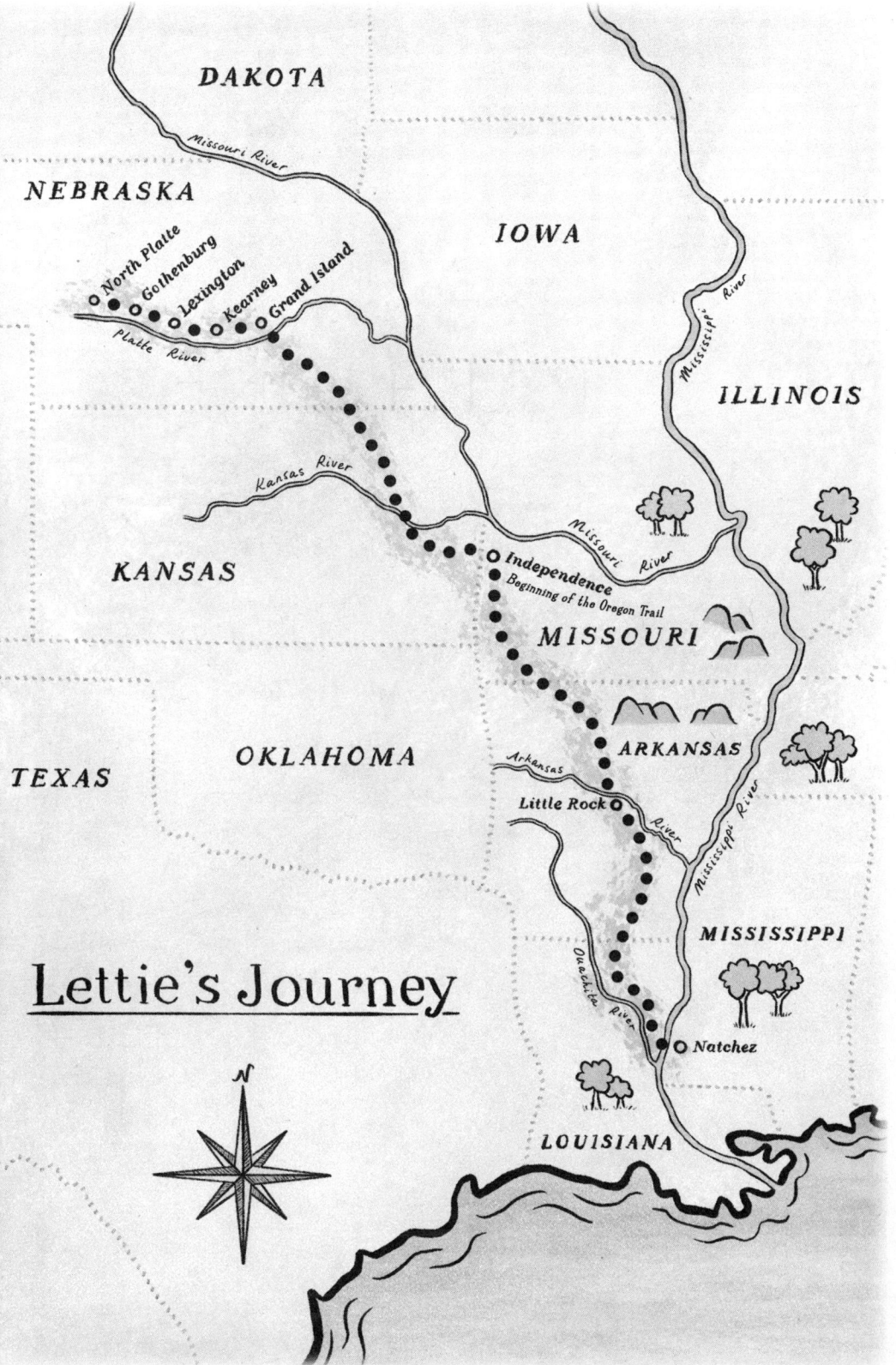

Lettie's Journey

PART ONE

· · · · · · · · · · · · · · · · ·

There was the story before we left

and the story after

but the story in between

is the part that's the hardest

—Lettie

Lettie

Natchez, Mississippi / February 1879

On the ride back from church
every time Charly
trotted faster
or trotted out the way
of a too-big hole in the road
my head fell against
Daddy's soft Sunday shirt
blue as a clear sky
Momma was humming
the hymns to herself
in the back of the wagon
we just finished
singing out loud
in the pews
Riding next to Daddy
listening to Momma
I asked Daddy
What was your momma and daddy like?
and he pulled back
hard on the reins
enough to make Charly start
and lift his head
wondering what Daddy wanted
Charly knew there wasn't no need
for Daddy to be pulling
in the middle of his trotting
in the middle of the road
when he knew just where he was going
Daddy heard my asking
but didn't answer straightaway
He stared over Charly's head
at the road home
instead of looking at me
like he always did when we talked
My momma's name was Hattie
He cleared his throat
And there wasn't a finer . . .
and cleared it again
Momma stopped her humming
There wasn't a finer woman in Louisiana
than my momma

I tried again
What was she like?
We rode on
bumping down the road

Finally Daddy said soft
Don't remember much of her
she was gone
when I was younger than you is now
but I remember her hands
They were always warm
and soft too
Hard as she worked
they stayed soft

What about your daddy?
I asked him again

That's enough questions now Lettie
Momma said from behind

But Daddy said
Nah
her asking is natural
Funny
don't remember my daddy
as much as I do my momma
They took him early one morning
He was there when I went to sleep
gone when I woke
We had to watch our momma
carry on working
caring for us
without our daddy
Acting
like it didn't matter to her none
He was sold off in the night
like he was nothing
to nobody
till they took her too
then
my two sisters
my baby sister one year
my older one the next

Whoa there
Daddy told Charly and Titus
in front of our cabin
My brothers
Elijah and Silas
jumped down from the wagon
racing each other
to the front door
Momma reached her hand to me
and I got down
but my daddy stayed sitting
his eyes closed now
I don't think it was because
he was trying to remember
what his momma and daddy were like
when he was young like me
I think it was because
he was trying
to not let me see him crying

Sylvia
Natchez, Mississippi / March 1879

He reached in his pocket
pulled out a paper
folded up small
Look like he been holding on to it for a time
Read it
Thomas told me

Took me a while to unfold
and read past the creases
What we know about Nebraska Thomas?

What it say there?
he asked
waiting on me to read it to him
Knew now some men told him
what the paper didn't

All the land you want
Free
he said to me

All we got to do is go on and get it
Take what's ours
I looked down at the paper
that didn't say none of what he was
Any colored who want it
Come with some money too right? I looked at his eyes
shining in the lamplight
bright
Who was I to dim their light?
To take from him what white men
masters
loss
and years of fieldwork left of him

He asked pointing down
at the paper
And they even give you a wagon?
Supplies?
He stood waiting

"SEE WHAT COLORED CITIZENS ARE DOING FOR THEIR
ELEVATION . . .
WHEREAS THE COLORED PEOPLE OF MISSISSIPPI
KNOWING THAT THERE IS AN ABUNDANCE OF CHOICE LANDS
NOW BELONGING TO THE GOVERNMENT
HAVE ASSEMBLED OURSELVES
FOR THE PURPOSE
OF LOCATING ON SAID LANDS . . ."

He was alive again
with hope
and I looked down
at the folded-up
creased-up paper in my hands
and started reading
some of what was written
and some
of what Thomas wanted to be

First time he came home from a meeting in town
look like he had a fever
Thomas?
I asked him

worried about the burning in his eyes
the sweat on his head
I had him sit to the table
You feeling all right?

I will be
he told me
I wet a cloth
pressed it to his head
before he pushed it away
We got to go West

Someone sick?
I asked him
Thinking he needed to see his people
he told me once were in Louisiana
Ain't no one sick
Ain't no one I need to see neither
I'm talking about West to Nebraska
Ain't nothing for us here

Before I could think
before I could make my tongue behave
I let it speak
Nebraska?
Natchez is our home Thomas!
We're free now
to live as we see fit

His eyes held the fire he was feeling inside
We can't live free
on someone else's land
picking someone else's crop!
I need something to call my own
Can't be no man
always waiting for someone to tell me
how much he gonna give
When
If
I made my tongue stay quiet this time
but he was done
his thundering over

5

Lettie

Natchez, Mississippi / April 1879

Momma
and Aunt Olivia
sent me outside
Go on and take Vivvy
they said
Get her some fresh air
But there wasn't no need
in sitting outside
on a day so damp
so cold
it hung
heavy on my dress
I tried walking her
around the yard the way she liked
pointing up high
at the pictures
in the clouds
Letting her pull moss
from the oaks
but quick snatching it back
before she shoved it
in her mouth
and laughing at her
laughing at squirrels
running every which way
But her shivering
took me back to the porch
and a chair
as close to the door
as I could get it
I held Vivvy in my arms

warming her
While I waited
I hummed silly songs
to quiet the shouting
coming from inside

Imma say what no one else will
Thomas was always
a damn fool

Even with my humming
and the creaking of the chair
outside
with me and Vivvy rocking
the shouting in Aunt Olivia's house
sounded like I was sitting
in the front pew
at Sunday service
and Uncle Benton was on the pulpit
trying to get his
lost sheep
he called them
like my daddy
who came to church but
never found their way to
being saved
accepting the Lord
getting baptized

Uncle Benton said again
Damn fool

Uncle Everett said
Now you ain't got to say all that Benton
Sylvia just talking

Then
my uncle Raleigh asked my momma
Thomas is not of a mind
to go dragging you all off to Nebraska
Ain't that right Sylvia?

I listened close
but when my momma didn't answer
Uncle Benton kept on

That is just what he's of a mind to do
and just like I said
Thomas was always a fool
and always will be
simple as that
moving West
ain't gonna change that fact

Lettie

Natchez, Mississippi / April 1879

The next night
after our day was done
while the beans and salt pork
greens and onions
were stewing in the pot for our supper
Daddy set us down
said he had something big
something important
he needed to tell us
Stop that shaking Silas
Daddy said
when he saw him wiggling
in his chair
But we were all just as wiggly
on the inside
as Silas was on the out
Momma sat next to me
and reached her hand
under the table
put it on mine when Daddy started talking
and telling us about moving

I sat quiet
listening to Daddy
but watching Momma
looking out the window
and over our heads
anywhere but in our eyes
Soon as Daddy finished talking
Elijah started fiddling
with his bootlaces
I kicked his leg under the table
Listen
I told him
*So you don't ask me
a hundred questions later*

Smart-mouthed he answered back
I am
When we coming back?

8

he asked Daddy
from moving I mean
I saw Momma's eyes fill up

Ain't no coming back once we leave 'lijah
Daddy told him

So why we leaving then?
Silas asked
Everything Elijah asked
Silas got to ask one question more

Now I just told y'all
Daddy took a long deep breath
started again
Out West
it gonna give us a chance to have me—
Daddy looked at Momma
Have us
some land of our own

Ain't that land of our own?
Elijah said
pointing through the window
to our plot out back

That ain't ours
Daddy said

Then why you plant on it
if it ain't ours?
Silas asked

Isn't Momma said to Silas
Isn't ours

Silas kept looking at Daddy
Daddy looked from Elijah
back to Silas
trying hard I could tell
to make us all understand
what was so plain to him
We just borrowing
from a white man

9

who owns it
But where we moving to
in Nebraska
we not gonna have to borrow
from a white man
We gonna have our own
Ain't that better than borrowing?

Isn't *it better*
Silas said to Daddy
smiling big at Momma
a big hole in his smile
where his front teeth was
just a week ago

Daddy kept talking
Always better to have your own
than to be asking someone
if you can have some of theirs
Y'all remember that now
Daddy stood up from the table
tired of all the explaining

10

Lettie
Natchez, Mississippi / May 1879

I thought there couldn't be nothing harder
than saying goodbye
to Aunt Olivia
and her husband Uncle Camp
my sweet baby cousin Vivvy
just now knowing me some
I could tell
because she waved her arms
every time I came near
and touched her nose
to mine
She pulled at my braids
hard
till I peeled her fingers apart
You are so strong Vivvy
I laughed
into her fat neck

She loves her big cousin
Aunt Olivia told me
I was gonna miss too
my uncles Benton, Everett, and Raleigh
and most of all
Oda
my friend
since we were *knee-high*
my momma told me
the kind of friends
that felt like
we had the same momma and daddy
The kind of friends
folks said
who even looked alike
When Momma told me
You'll have someone to write to
once you get to Nebraska
You can tell Oda
all about what it's like there

I asked Momma
my words
salty
as smoked ham
How is sending a letter
anything near the same
as being with her
and playing school
the way we do
Oda is about the only friend
I ever had
aside from Charly
and you and Daddy
are taking me away from her
Momma paid no mind
to my back talk
Instead
she pulled me close
and wiped my face
dry
with her apron
from the tears
that just wouldn't stop

Lettie
Natchez, Mississippi / May 1879

Almost as hard
as the goodbyes
was all the packing we had to do
kettles
pots
lifting
hauling
Elijah and Silas
doing less than they should
or could
but enough
so Momma and Daddy were too busy
to pay them any mind
Seems like they already forgot
we're moving away
far from home to a place neither ever heard of
and not much
is likely gonna be the same again
Momma said Elijah and Silas
were too young to understand

You gotta try and help 'em Lettie
but I was trying to make it clear
in my own head
Course, it was all
Get a move on Lettie
and *Girl, I know you can move faster than that*
from Daddy
Nothing from Momma
not one word
when I packed in her sewing basket
shawls
a jar of buttons
the mixing bowl her momma gave her
that she never let me touch
even when we baked a cake
for Christmas
But when I handed Silas's cradle to Daddy
to put in the back of our wagon
Ain't gonna need that where we going

Daddy said
and handed it back to me
I brought it back to the house
and set it outside the door
hoping Momma wouldn't see just yet
but she did and said
Lettie, I told you to put that on the wagon
with the rest of our things

But Daddy—
I started to say
Momma looked past the door
at Daddy up on the wagon
the knowing on her face
then looked at me and the cradle
and kept on packing
faster now
slamming clothes
and whatever else she could find
in our trunks
and went on back
to saying not one word more

Lettie
Natchez, Mississippi / May 1879

I kept my eyes closed tight
but sleep wouldn't come
I listened to Daddy's snoring
from the small bed
I shared
in the loft up above
the big room down below

I watched Silas
his thumb in his mouth
Everyone who saw Silas
soaked in the sweetness of him
Now you know
he is too pretty to be a boy
they told Daddy
Or

If I didn't have enough of my own
I'd surely bring that boy home with me
cute as he is
they said to Momma
and she'd laugh and say
You'd turn him right back to me
soon as you got him home
She was tickled
anyone could see
Except one day we were in town
and a white woman
slowed
when we walked past
and said to Momma
staring down at Silas
I'd sure love to have that boy
and Momma picked up Silas fast
big as he was
and said
Thank you kindly ma'am
He's my sweet boy
Isn't that right Silas?
We went straight home after that
Momma wouldn't let Silas go
even when he told Momma
I wanna walk Momma

and when I asked
What about the things we needed
at the store?

Momma said
I'll send your daddy later
Let's just get on home

I watched him now
sweet
breathing soft as a whisper
and Elijah
tossing and kicking the way he did
always like he was fighting
to keep sleep away
The owls
mockingbirds

katydids
all stayed wide awake
with me
and kept my mind on
the miles
and I didn't know how many towns
we'd travel through
how many people
we'd pass by
on our way to Nebraska
I wondered what I'd hear
in a different place
every night
in tents
or in our wagon
wrapped in blankets
under a sky that stretched
all the way from Mississippi
West

Sylvia
Natchez, Mississippi / May 1879

Lord grant them traveling grace
as they travel these roads
And Lord . . .
My head was bowed
Thomas squeezed my hand tight
so I opened my eyes
to see his one foot tapping
in the dirt
in front of our wagon
while Benton prayed over us
I squeezed his hand back
In your precious name
Amen
Thomas climbed up
while my family gathered round
Benton handed me his Bible

We ain't got no room for books
Thomas yelled down from his seat

Always room for the Good Book
Benton said right back
pressing the Bible in my hands
I held it
as tight as my family held me
until Thomas yelled
Sylvia!
and I climbed up
to join one family
while I left the other
behind

Lettie
Natchez, Mississippi / May 1879

Starting out
I sat up front next to my daddy
behind our mules Charly and Titus
where I could smell their sweat
and watch their tails
flipping from side to side
aching to get a move on
and I could
watch my daddy's dry hands
hold tight to the reins
driving them to our new home
I waved goodbye
to everyone we passed
standing along the road
out of town
The Haskins
smiled from their doorway
Mr. Robbins was in his front yard
fixing his fence
but looked up
nodded his goodbye
and then we passed Oda's house
where she stood out on the road
waiting
Lettie!
she shouted
Lettie!

As we neared
I stopped my waving
and stared down
my arm now too heavy to lift
Oda!
I shouted back
and then our wagon passed by
slow
and Oda was gone
When there was no folks left
I lifted my arm
and waved again
to everything else I was leaving
the dogwoods
hickory
and oak trees
the buds of clover
and wildflowers
along the side of the road
budding now in the spring
The cows
horses
and sheep chewing grass in the fields
till Daddy said
Stop that fuss now
with no mad in his voice
Up front next to Daddy
I'd be able to see
where we were going
once we got on our way
and count the miles
in my head
like I counted out the supplies
Daddy bought for us
200 pounds of flour
10 pounds of rice
5 pounds of coffee
25 pounds of sugar
1 bushel of beans
20 pounds of salt
1 bushel of cornmeal
1 keg of vinegar
100 pounds of bacon

25 pounds of dried fruit
Daddy's good rifle and gunpowder
two pistols
lard, candles, lye powder
matches and soap
frying pans and a coffeepot
our old stew kettle and Momma's sharpest knife
nails
one washtub
A tent and blankets
blankets for Charly and Titus
plus their feed too
even the cradle Momma wanted
was packed in tight
I wrote it all down in a book
like Momma whispered I should
so I could add up the numbers
and remind Daddy
how much we paid
and how much we had left to spend for our move
West
The way Daddy said it
sounded like there wasn't no place
I'd rather be
except it was hard
to feel the free
Daddy said I was supposed to be feeling
listening to my brothers Silas and Elijah
with their shouting and wrestling
and the huffing
of Charly and Titus
and pretend
in the back of our wagon
I didn't hear my momma crying

Lettie
Natchez, Mississippi / May 1879

We didn't have far to ride
when we left out
and said our goodbyes
Just down
to the water

in Natchez
to the riverfront
and the dock
where the steamships would come
Daddy said
that would take us
and our wagon
all the way up the Mississippi River
to a city called St. Louis
I figured Uncle Benton
had to like that city
because it sounded
like a place
that might be
filled
with the kind of holy folks
he'd like
saints

We gonna walk
rest of the way
West
Daddy told me

How far is that gonna be?
Walking from St. Louis
to Nebraska?
I asked Daddy

Far enough
he told me

And I knew that meant
he wasn't so sure
himself
I'd been to the river
plenty of times
every summer
on revival Sundays
when Uncle Benton
baptized anyone who needed saving
I was so scared
on the Sunday
he baptized me

I nearly tripped on the long
white robe
Momma dressed me in
that morning
Uncle Benton
folded my hands
across my chest
before he laid me back
quick
in the water
while everyone stood
on the banks
singing
Take me to the water
to be baptized . . .
None but the righteous
shall see God . . .

And then I was all wet
and coughing up water
Born again
in Christ
Uncle Benton said
But I didn't feel
Reborn
Washed clean
of my sin
like Uncle Benton
told everyone
standing on the riverbank
watching me
and clapping
I just felt wet

Sylvia
Natchez, Mississippi / May 1879

Thomas had us wait
with the wagon
while he went to go find Mr. Casey
and the others
we were meant to travel with
Folks looked like

they'd been there
for days
just worn out

How long y'all been here?
I asked the young woman
sitting next to us
her husband snoring soft
beside her on a blanket
She laughed

Two
Three days maybe

And no ships come
in three days?
I asked her

Didn't say that
The woman yawned big
They just ain't letting
us on

How long
you plan on waiting?

She smiled
back at me
Long as we have to
she said
and laid down
alongside
her husband
and closed her eyes

Silas and Elijah
sat under our wagon
paying no mind
to anything
or anyone
but their own foolin'
and fussin'
while me and Lettie
watched

and waited
for Thomas
and the steamships
next to the woman
and her snoring husband

Lettie
Natchez, Mississippi / May 1879

I found them
Daddy told us
All of them
sitting just over there

Daddy pointed
past a group of wagons
Amos
his sons
Didn't expect
to see the Days
their boy and girl
look to be 'bout Lettie's age
Sylvia they asking after you
whole lot of others
I don't know

Momma looked
to where Daddy
was pointing
Told me
to bring y'all over
We all wait together
Make sure we
get on the same ship
all at one time

When is the next one coming?
Momma asked

Mr. Casey expecting
should be right along soon
Said last two were filled

but we bound to get
on the next
or else we gonna have to swim
right Lettie?
Daddy laughed
putting his arm around me

We gonna swim all the way?
Silas yelled
from under the wagon

You can't swim from here
Elijah shouted at him

Daddy is just making fun
I told him
nicer
so he wouldn't start
his crying
Daddy lifted them both
up from under
and into the bed of the wagon

But . . .
Momma said soft
just to Daddy
You sure they stopping
for us?

Course they is
Daddy laughed
Long as we got our fare
we passengers
like everyone else

Get on up here Lettie
he told me
patting the seat beside him
He grabbed the reins
and Charly and Titus
started forward
By the time we reached
Mr. Casey and all the folks

23

we were traveling with
I had barely
started counting
the faces I knew
Before I heard the ship coming
and folks screaming
Here it is
and rushing past us
loaded down
just like us
with everything they owned
wagons
animals
chairs and tables
pots and pans
Shouting
Hurry now
the ship is here

Our whole group
turned toward the river
making our way too
in the crowd
looking toward the ship
moving fast
but not so fast
I couldn't see the faces
on the deck
at the rails
were white folks
talking
smiling
on board
Some waved
Some stared
but the boat kept moving
fast
faster
even though
everyone around us
was shouting
Wait!
Stop!
Don't leave us . . .

What in the devil . . .
I heard someone
in our group
say behind me

What is going on?
Momma said soft
to herself

Is that our boat Momma?
Silas was pulling on
Momma's arm now

Come here Silas
I told him
taking his hand
There's another boat
coming for us
soon
right Daddy?
I asked
wanting to know too

Daddy shook his head
Yes
Slow
saying nothing
still looking
where everyone else
was too
at the water
where the boat passed
with people
standing on board
at the deck
and rails
but plenty of room still
for us
the colored passengers
left behind
in Natchez

Lettie

Natchez, Mississippi / May 1879

Daddy came back
to the wagon
just when the sun was going down
after being gone for hours
with Mr. Casey
and some other men
in our group
Momma
had just pulled out
cold biscuits and ham
wrapped in cloth from a basket
for our supper
Daddy was out of breath
like he'd been running

Got a new plan
Daddy said fast
to Momma
and he pulled Momma
to the side of the wagon
He put his hands
on Momma's shoulders
and leaned in close
talking soft
Momma stood
listening
with her arms
lying
stiff and straight
down by her side
Daddy came back
and told us
Time we get a move on

He didn't wait
for Silas
to start his asking
Just climbed up into the wagon
and I climbed up
next to him

watching him
keep his eyes
on Charly and Titus
Finally I asked the question
Silas would have

Where we going Daddy?

We going West Lettie
just like I said

But everybody
is waiting for the boats
back there
I pointed behind us

You ain't never
gonna get nowhere in life Lettie
You always worried
'bout what everyone else is doing
Sometimes you got to do things
your own way
to get ahead
Daddy said

Sylvia
Crossing the Mississippi River to Louisiana / May 1879

Trust me
is what Thomas told me
when he said
we weren't going to take the steamship
to St. Louis

Too many people
Too much money
Mr. Casey got a better plan
he told me

And so now
in the dark of the night
Instead of heading north

upriver
We're crossing west
by flatboat
just across the river
to Louisiana
then making our way
on foot
up to Missouri
and West

It's gonna be faster this way
faster than waiting
and hoping to get a boat
ain't no need
to spend up all we have
on fare
when we all got feet
for walking
that don't cost us nothing
Thomas told me

I looked at Thomas
and thought
of my brother Benton
and his words
when I told him we were leaving
moving West

Searching for some Promised Land
he called it out West
Ain't no reason
Y'all can't find what you're looking for
right here
Freedom found us
No doubt
more good is coming this way
for coloreds
When he pulled me close
at our wagon
saying goodbye
he whispered hard in my ear
Thomas thinking
he leading you
to some Promised Land

but sister
you gotta be your own
Moses now

Lettie
Crossing the Mississippi River to Louisiana / May 1879

Titus is always scared
of one thing
or the next
So Daddy had me
stand next to him
on the ride over
across on the boat
the water splashing up high
Against the boat
rocking fast
As the currents
pulled us one way
the men steering the boat
pulled us another
I kept my hand on Titus's back
saying soft over
and over again
Hold still there Titus
Hold still
Charly was on his other side
calm as could be
like it was every day
he crossed the Mississippi
readying to make his way
West
Titus marched in place
snorting
He didn't want no part
and I kept rubbing
and saying soft
Hold still
We almost there
till the boat
slowed its rocking
and we were
on the other side

Sylvia
Vidalia, Louisiana / May 1879

Reaching the other side
of the river
just meant we needed
to wait some more
through the night
for the others
to break down their wagons
and load them on
to get across
and unload them
and rebuild the wagons
on the other side
and then to rest
and then
like Thomas and the men planned
to start moving on foot
to Missouri
and the Oregon Trail west
to Nebraska

There were nearly as many here
on the Louisiana side
of the river
as there were
on the Mississippi side
looking just as tired
and wishing
just as hard
that surely the next boat
would stop
for them
Part of me
wanted to stay and wait
with them
not be in any hurry
to leave
and part of me
wanted to get going
so I wouldn't have to see
the hurt
of folks standing on the banks

holding all they had
hopes
and dreams
only to have them
left behind
when the ships came again
and didn't stop

Lettie
Louisiana / May 1879

I couldn't decide where I wanted to be
up front next to
Daddy
or in back
under the pretty white cover
that Daddy stretched over our wagon
like a wide round roof
and fastened down tight with rope
Daddy said it would keep us dry from the wet
warm from the cold
and cool from the sun
How one white cloth
could do all that
I didn't rightly know
but Daddy sounded so sure
I believed him
With all our food packed in a box in the wagon bed
fastened in front behind the seat
our chests of clothes and blankets on one side
Elijah and Silas playing marbles
on the other
laid out on the straw mattress
There was hardly any room for me to sit
in back
even if I wanted to
so I sat up front with Daddy
Momma didn't mind
she said
and I could tell
she meant it

Sylvia
Louisiana / May 1879

Four months
is what Thomas told me
Maybe five
If we get held up
Six at the most
is the time it would take
to get us to Nebraska
months
of road
and field
and towns

We hadn't traveled
not one day
and already
I was too tired to move
Walking the roads
hurt my feet
Sitting in the wagon
hurt my backside
Our home now
wasn't nothing
but a wagon
and our trunks
for four
five
six months
So I sat
my backside hurting
watching Silas and Elijah
listening to Thomas and Lettie
heading forward
but looking back

Lettie
Louisiana / May 1879

I counted six wagons in front of us
three in back
ten of us in all

four of the families
we knew from town
The Caseys, the Bakers, the Days
Mrs. Clara Spruill and my momma would pass
the time every so often
She was traveling with her husband William
and mother *Mrs. Lucinda Abrams*
She said her own name proud
though everyone I knew
called her Miss Lucy
She was old but strong too
Momma told me she said
Imma walk all the way West
if I have to
for a piece of land
to finally call my own
Mr. Amos Casey
and his boys Beau and Emmanuel
both taller now than their daddy
had a wagon so big
they had a team of oxen
to pull it
plus one milk cow and a sheep
when most everybody else
just had their mules
Daddy told me once
Was Mr. Casey
gave me a chance
when no one else round here would
He's the kind of man
don't need to make other folks feel small
to show how big he is
I never knew quite what Daddy meant
but I knew
Daddy liked him
and if Daddy liked him
then I did too
Daddy said
as much as Mr. Casey had here
land
animals
he was thinking
out West
a man with good business sense
could have even more

And that's the type of man
your daddy aims to be
he said
The Day family
had the daddy Marshall
his wife Anne
and their boy and girl
Earl and Agnes
I'd seen
in the older class at school
There was Bruin and Dottie Baker
and their baby girl
cute almost as Vivvy
But everyone else
we didn't know
Everyone took the time
telling their names to each other
Momma pushed me forward
so I could say mine
I'm Lettie
I felt like I said
about a hundred times

34

That's a pretty name
or
pretty name for a pretty girl
just about everybody said
That told me they were nice folks
going along with us
We met
Jackson and Pleasant Lorton
and their two girls
Eliza and Hester
years younger than my brothers
and two boys bigger
Presley and Duke
I could tell right off Elijah and Silas
would be following those boys
every chance they got
Then it was Merritt Boston
his wife Lydia
too sickly to even rise
from her pallet in back of their wagon
and their grown girls

Arlene, Ellen, and Heloise
Butch and Odette Anderson
who never let go
of each other's hands
and said they were married
just a week ago over in Vicksburg
by her granddaddy
Two brothers Hark and Oscar Cole
The older one Hark
standing a head taller
than his brother
They were older than my daddy
but still looked strong and steady
and an old man
named Mr. Tom Portee
traveling with just his small beat-up wagon
and his old dog
I always wanted a dog
but it was the one thing
that no matter how many times I asked
Daddy always said
No
When I said hello to Mr. Portee
his dog limped over
and sniffed my feet
What's your name boy?
I said to him
scratching behind
his pointy ears
He looked up at me
with wet
sweet
brown eyes

Name's Sutter
Mr. Portee said
and Sutter came closer
and laid his head
of patchy fur
against my leg
like he knew me his whole life

You're a good boy Sutter
I can tell

I told him
I rubbed the fur down
on top of his head
sticking up
every which way

He sure is
Ain't you boy?
Mr. Portee said

I knelt down close

And my Sutter
is a good judge of character
He ain't never been wrong
far as I can tell
Mr. Portee told me
smiling big
and I saw
he was missing his front teeth
just like Silas

Lettie
Louisiana / May 1879

After we got settled into camp
the first night
Daddy told me to eat up quick
He went in the wagon
and changed
into his clean
sky-blue
Sunday shirt from the trunk
came back and asked
How do I look?

Silas shouted
Like yourself
and that got Elijah
and Silas both to laughing
Daddy looked to me
and Momma

I said
Handsome Daddy
like I knew
he was hoping to hear
and Momma wasn't saying
Daddy told me early on
before we camped
that tonight
would be the voting
where everyone
had to pick
who they wanted
for company Captain
to lead us
General
to plan out the route we'd follow
Commander
to keep order
and for a Major
to do everything else I guess

Which job do you want Daddy?
I asked him

Ain't no better job than the Captain Lettie
Course, I'll take General too
Either one means you leading
And that's what I was meant to do
I heard Momma start humming
from inside the wagon

We'll all vote for you
I told him

Daddy looked down at me
You got to be grown to vote baby

Well Momma will then
That's one vote
I smiled at him

Daddy patted my head
soft

Grown men Lettie
Women don't vote
I thought on that
when I gathered up sticks
and dry brush
for the fire with Elijah
I thought of another question
for Daddy
Why don't women get to decide
who leads them
and plans their route
and keeps order?

Daddy said
That's why women
have husbands Lettie
so they ain't got to do the choosing
Men provide for them
keep them safe
Once you grown
you'll see for yourself
how lucky you are
to have you a husband

Lettie
Louisiana / May 1879

My daddy told me he never got a chance
to fight in the war
like he wanted to
They never came recruiting
down near Louisiana
he said
But he told me he wanted to fight
beside the Union boys
from up North
I would have put a hurtin'
on every Confederate soldier
I had a mind to
Daddy told me
raising his fists at me
like he was already fighting
When the voting started up

My brothers
And the Lorton children
took off playing
by themselves
but not me
I stood near the women
watching
The women didn't raise their hands
to vote
but I think they still were
voting
by themselves

Nearly every man raised their hand
for Mr. Casey as our company Captain
except my daddy
He told me before the voting started
he'd be just as good a leader
as Mr. Casey
probably better
Just 'cause you got money
don't make you no leader
Don't make you better neither

I know Daddy
I told him
So now
It was Mr. Casey's job
to give the word
when it was time to leave
and when it was time to stop
and water and feed the mules and oxen
or have meetings to discuss
what needed discussing

After the vote
where only men
could do the choosing
we all watched
when they chose
Daddy
to be the Major
in our company
not the Captain

or the General
like he wanted
Walking back to our wagon
Daddy told me
Being a Major
means Imma keep watch at night
Make sure y'all safe

From animals?
I asked him

Well, yes
Daddy said slow
and whatever else be roaming
out there at night
trying to snatch up my little girl!
He grabbed me
in a hug
and held me tight
And he didn't seem
nearly as sad
as he looked
when I saw
his face after hands were raised
for others
and not for him
and not nearly as mad
as he sounded
when I heard him
shouting to Momma later
They gonna treat me like a man
and Momma hushed him saying
Quiet now Thomas
all that fussing
gonna wake the children
But I was already awake
listening
and keeping an account
of their words
in my book of numbers

40

Sylvia
Louisiana / May 1879

When I gave Lettie
a book for keeping our numbers

She did us proud
writing in her best hand
making sure
there wasn't nothing
gonna be missed
She better with numbers
than most men
smarter too
Thomas said to me at night
I told him
My sister Olivia is the same way
good at her numbers—
Thomas kept on
If her brothers are anywhere near
as smart as my Lettie
There ain't nothing . . .
Thomas always say
My Lettie
My
My
Like she's all his
Our Lettie
is good at most things
smart as she is
I seen her
playing teacher
with her friend Oda
spelling out words
on her slate
I knew then
that's just what our Lettie's
gonna be someday
a teacher
I know too
the only person
Thomas trusts more than hisself
is Lettie

PART TWO

· · · · · · · · · · · · ·

Ain't that a man
Always got to go chasing
'cause he can't never see
what's right before his eyes

—Sylvia

Sylvia
Louisiana / May 1879

Me and my sister Olivia
brothers
each one of us know this land
like it was family
Our feet
our hands
walked and held the soil
that fed us
grew us up
It was where our momma and daddy
worked for nothing
Then when freedom came
not much more than nothing
It spoke to us
We can smell when a soaking rain is coming
from how far off
Know when we're going to make a good crop
Know when we're not
Thomas never knew the land like that
Came to it by way of need
not want
The land knows you my daddy used to say
Treat it right
It'll take care of you all your days
miss my daddy every day
But I sure am glad he's not here
to see how Thomas
curses the heat
the weevils
Don't listen to what the land
or no one else neither
is telling him
So every season
when crops are ripe
and there's a bounty
we still struggling to get ours in
because he overplanted
or harvested too late
and some lay in the fields dying
wasting back to the land they sprung from

him cursing all the while
swearing
it's *Mississippi land*
White men
Bad luck
Sometimes *me*
not believing in him
that's making living hard for us
and easy for everyone else
Can't hear the land in Mississippi
How's he gonna hear it
in Nebraska?

Lettie
Louisiana / May 1879

Roll out!
The call came
from Mr. Casey at the front
our Captain
and one after the other we left out

Our wagon
could barely hold us five
and all we brought
Where we gonna sleep?
Elijah asked
when Daddy showed him
inside
after we were all packed up
and ready to leave Natchez
What you mean
where we gonna sleep?
We sleeping under
an open sky boy

Silas started crying then
We sleeping outside?
In the dirt?
he asked
Momma held him close
and looked at Daddy

her lips tight
You'll have a tent
and a nice warm fire
and Lettie and Elijah
beside you
like always
she said soft
in his ear

Daddy knelt down to Silas
What your momma's telling y'all is
we ain't got much
but we got all we need
till we get West
and build us a great big house
bigger than this one here
Daddy pointed to our cabin
plus
I got my rifle to catch us anything we need to eat

I put my hand in Silas's
And we got God too right Daddy?
Because that was what Uncle Benton told Momma
last Sunday after supper
and we were saying our goodbyes
You'll need God guiding you every step of the way
Otherwise—

Stop it now Benton
Momma shushed him
Just let it be

But instead of Daddy saying
Yep Lettie, God on our side is just what we need
or
Baby girl, we got God right here beside us
Daddy grunted
got up into the wagon seat
and said down to me
You, your momma, and your brothers got me
your daddy
and that's all you gonna need to make it
to Nebraska

Titus huffed
Charly puffed

Lettie
Louisiana and crossing into Arkansas / May 1879

Too hot today
to sit in the wagon where it heated up
so much
Momma said
she felt like she was a hot biscuit
It was the first time I seen her smile
since we left home
twelve days ago
We all had to walk now
to save Charly and Titus
from pulling extra
We were hoping for a breeze
but the sun and
sticky heat
and roads

muddy from last night's rain
slowed down even my brothers
from chasing each other
and the grasshoppers and butterflies
through the fields
we walked through
the soft grass under our feet
easier than the hard
rutted roads
the wagons traveled

I held Momma's hand tight
slippery with her sweat
with our other hands
we waved away
the mosquitos that followed

in black clouds above us
like they were traveling West too
We couldn't talk
or we'd swallow

them whole
Instead
I had to think quiet about
the leaves of magnolia and sweet gum trees
and the smell of the honeysuckle we passed
and the way the ground
sometimes went from
rocks
to mud
back again to rocks
Mr. Spruill
said we were crossing into Arkansas
and I covered my mouth
from the mosquitos
to tell Momma
how once
when we were studying maps in school
I asked my teacher Miss Rowser
why one state was named *Kansas*
and the other
who was its neighbor
was named *Ar-Kansas*
Did someone run out of names?
and Miss Rowser laughed so hard
I thought she'd bust
She told the class
Lettie made a good observation
But it is pronounced Ar-Kan-Saw
which didn't make any kind of sense to me
So I still call it *Ar-Kansas* to myself
But I didn't tell Momma that last part
I squeezed Momma's hand
wondering if she was listening
wondering why she didn't laugh
like Miss Rowser did
wondering why she didn't squeeze my hand back
I hoped it was just because
she didn't want
a mouthful of mosquitos

Lettie
Arkansas / May 1879

There was a rip
in the corner
of our tent
and each morning
that is where
pink sky
waited to peek in
and be the first to call me awake
like Momma did back home
I slipped on my dress
and tied my boots
and stepped quiet over
still sleeping
Silas and Elijah
I scooped the dipper
in our water bucket
hanging off the side of
our wagon
and poured the cold water into
my hands
to clean off
the dust and dirt
from my face
I dipped one more scoop
to wet my mouth
and walked a ways
from the tents and our wagon
to sit
and wait for the sun
to wake up the whole sky
Momma and Daddy
Silas and Elijah
Charly and Titus
and the rest of the camp
The back of my dress
was wet
from the rock
where I sat
I heard sniffing
behind me

and I turned
Mr. Portee's dog
Sutter
was poking his nose around
in some grass
And Lord knows what else

C'mere boy
I held out my hand
He stood still
deciding
and then came over
sniffed me too
and licked my hand
my knee
my neck
His fur
was as wet as my dress
He must have had
someplace to be
because he trotted off
after a while
Two rabbits
ran past
racing each other
the way Silas and Elijah do
and a hawk
flew overhead
already up
looking for a breakfast
of rabbits

Lettie
Arkansas / May 1879

Standing tall
up above
the Arkansas River
was the Baring Cross Bridge
Daddy told me
but he only said the name
when he cussed it

and the people
standing in the booth at the end
waiting to collect money
Tolls
They told us
we needed to pay
to cross with our wagons
to get over to the other side of the river
Momma took out our tin
and had me count out the coins we needed
and write them down in the book
They own all the land
and the river too?
Daddy shouted words
Momma said
no man who knows his Bible
ought to be shouting
I heard Elijah and Silas
laughing soft in back
and I had to cover my mouth
to stop myself from smiling too
One by one
our company crossed

The river looked prettier
standing on top of it
Daddy made Silas and Elijah
stay inside the wagon
afraid
like we all were
they would fall
into the water below
for looking
but he let me walk
Real careful now Lettie
he told me
near the edge
on the new smooth wooden floor
at the river below
laid out calm and still
like a blanket at a picnic
Between one bank
and the other

Daddy had to talk nice to Titus
Getting him to keep his eyes
straight ahead
and not look to the side
or down
lest he get scared
Even with me taking my time
it didn't take long to cross
Even though Daddy was mad
about paying money to cross
I thought it was worth
every cent

I tried counting
all the miles
we walked
and rode so far
in my head
guessing partly by the time we kept
with the sun
Two miles an hour
Mr. Spruill
our General
who maps our route
told me
is about the best we can do

That's all?
I asked him
knowing Daddy told me
when we started out
We need to cover
'bout twenty miles a day
if we gonna make it to Nebraska
'fore the cold sets in
Any less than that
we in trouble

Mr. Casey
had a special tool
fastened good to his wagon wheel
to keep count of the miles we traveled
every day

You our roadometer
Daddy told me laughing
I trust you
more than some old machine
Daddy was right
Somehow
I kept up with the miles
just as good
as Mr. Casey's roadometer
Think we did
about ten so far today
I told Momma
almost half the miles
we needed every day
to make it before the snow
I'm almost wishing for now
It's so hot
Me and Momma watched my brothers
joining up with Presley and Duke
the Lorton boys
You'll need to keep an eye on them
Momma told me
or they'll get into something
they can't get out of

Yes ma'am
I said

When we stopped to camp
Daddy walked with Mr. Day
and I saw his hands making shapes
in the sky
over his head
and we knew he was talking about all the land
all the freedom
all the money
ahead
like if Mr. Day just looked close
he could see what Daddy saw
up above
in the sky
I wondered if that's what Uncle Benton
and Momma meant

when I heard them say
Daddy's head
was always in the clouds

Lettie
Arkansas / May 1879

After the sun went down
and we stopped to set up camp
I kissed Charly and Titus good night
and then we gathered our wagons in a circle
to keep the animals
we traveled with
in
and the animals who hunt them
out
Daddy started a fire
Momma unloaded her pots
and started on supper
we ate
hot biscuits
using them to scoop up Momma's beans
soon as they hit our bowls
When we finished
Daddy went to join the other men
who sat smoking by a fire in front of Mr. Day's wagon
Their voices turned from whispers
to loud talking
to shouting
and Daddy came back
looking mad
saying to Momma
They gonna treat me like a man
not some child who
don't know what he's talking about

Momma nodded slow
What happened Thomas?
Kept up her scrubbing the cooking pot
I got our bedrolls ready
in the tent
and called in Silas and Elijah

So far
the best part of traveling West
was the nighttime
and feeling like
wherever I laid my head
at night
was all mine
I could lay out my blankets
in front of a fire
that kept away snakes
Far enough away from my brothers
away from their tossing and turning
and stinking feet
listening to the night sounds
owls and cicadas
wolves and coyote
I heard Mr. Day
telling his wife
their loud yapping
kept him up
near half the night
Sometimes

If it was warm enough
I liked to sleep
under one big open sky
It felt like my arms could stretch
all the way
from Mississippi to Nebraska
and there would still be room enough
if I wanted
to stretch out some more
Tonight
I laid under my blanket
watching the dark sky above
Daddy's head was maybe
in the clouds
but mine
was in the stars

Lettie
Arkansas / June 1879

Help me get these tents folded
Momma told me this morning
soon as I got up
Where's Daddy?

Didn't ask for your questions Lettie
just asked for your help
Momma said
But as soon as we finished folding
I went over to the wagon
where I could hear Daddy's heavy breathing
Sleeping
Let him be
Momma told me
There was no more pink
in the sky
so it was too late
for Daddy to be sleeping
when all the wagons were packed
and Mr. Casey
was ready to call us out
Miss Clara came over
asking Momma
You all right here Sylvia?
William says we can't wait no more
we gonna keep time
But maybe if Thomas . . .
I saw her look at the wagon
I could ask . . .
Saw her look to where Daddy
was sleeping still
alone
at us still eating
our warmed-over breakfast
of last night's beans
Momma whispered in her ear
the way I used to with Oda
and Miss Clara nodded her head
up and down
Well . . .

all right then
her hand slipped in Momma's
squeezed it tight
like Oda squeezed mine
and I looked into the fire
thinking again about
me and Oda
and wondering
whose hand
she was holding now

We're just fine here
We'll catch up to you at the next stop
Momma told Miss Clara
If you're sure . . .
Miss Clara said
moving away and letting go
of Momma's hand

Lettie
Arkansas / June 1879

I couldn't see the company ahead
so I knew we wouldn't catch up
anytime soon
but I hoped we'd see them all
at the next stop
We safer in numbers
Daddy told me
when we first started out
and I asked Daddy
why there were so many of us
traveling together
But Daddy isn't saying much now
sitting up front
quiet
while we walk
on land stretched before us
just as dry as we are
our one wagon
and us five
all alone

Lettie
Arkansas / June 1879

Today the roads
were easier
They were mostly smoothed-down dirt
worn from wagon wheels
and hooves
with more houses
set along the road
some pretty ones
built strong
and straight
not like ours back home
that always looked
like the roof was off to one side
the way Elijah's head tilted over
when he was fixing to ask me a question
We needed those smooth
worn-down roads
and straight path
to catch the others as quick as we did
I liked to think
they waited longer than they should have
for us
down at the day's resting spot
a small gully
under the shade of a tree

There you are
Miss Clara shouted
when she saw Momma
late in the day
She took off her big hat
and her bright smile
almost made me forget
how scared
I'd been feeling all day
thinking about being
left behind
being alone
with a momma and daddy

who didn't do as much talking
as they used to
two brothers
who didn't do enough listening
Charly and Titus
who seemed more tired than ever
and me
who was starting to wonder
if I'd rather
be back home in Natchez
with Oda and everyone I knew
or here
going on ahead to
Nebraska

That night
all of us
and Charly and Titus
were tireder
than ever
from walking too fast
trying to catch up to the others
hardly stopping to rest
Silas and Elijah
were already sleeping
without even putting up a fuss
when Momma
peeled them apart
and stripped them
out of their dirty underdrawers

I wanted to be asleep too
but I heard Momma and Daddy
behind our wagon
Don't make you no less of a man
to make what's wrong right
We can't do this alone Thomas
least I can't
'specially not now . . .

Wasn't too often Daddy had nothing to say
but all I could hear
was Momma talking
and Daddy huffing and puffing

like Charly when he was tired
I heard Daddy get up
and walk away
I figured mad enough
to sleep again
in the wagon
alone
but instead
Daddy made his way over
to Mr. Day's wagon
where the men were already sitting
talking and laughing and such
Seemed the whole camp was quiet
waiting
and watching
I moved my bedroll
so my head
was poking out of my tent
Daddy sat on a log by hisself
staring at the fire
until one of Mr. Casey's sons
Emmanuel I think it was
offered Daddy his pipe
Much obliged
I made out
for the pipe I'm guessing
but I know he meant for the kindness too
and next thing I heard was music
a fiddle
and a deep voice singing
hands clapping
my daddy laughing
and my momma
humming along

Lettie
Arkansas / June 1879

Twenty-nine days
we've been walking
to Nebraska
and today
when we stopped

by a creek
with just enough
water above its muddy bottom
to water the animals
I ate up my dried beef
and corn cake
and heard the loud laughing
of my brothers and their
new friends
over behind a sycamore
its thick trunk
nearly hiding them
When I got up to see
what they were doing
I saw Presley
the younger Lorton boy
throwing rocks
Your turn
he told Elijah
putting a rock in his hand
I walked over
and saw they were standing
a ways from Sutter
Mr. Portee's dog
who was shaking
too scared to run

You throwing rocks
at Sutter?
I yelled
snatching the rock from Elijah
but shouting down at Presley
He turned to run
but I grabbed hold of him

You ever so much as
go near that dog again . . .
I looked at all four of them

He ain't your dog!
Duke
the other Lorton boy yelled
mean in his eyes
So it ain't your concern

Isn't
yelled Silas
looking at me
then Duke
wanting to say something
but not sure what
Isn't *her concern*
Silas
said soft
to hisself more than anyone else

We don't go around hurting
things
people or animals
whether they're ours or not
I yelled

Elijah nodded his head
Silas looked down
but Duke stared right back at me
When I let Presley go
the boys ran off
Sutter too

That night when we camped
I went looking for Sutter
who was lapping up
muddy water from a puddle
That's gonna make you sick Sutter
I told him
and he stopped his drinking
and came over
slow
I fed him a piece of beef I saved
for him
and his wet mouth
made a mess of it in my hand
You stay clear of those Lorton boys
you hear me?
I told him
His wet eyes
looked at me
and told me
he knew to be more careful next time

I gave him one good scratching
behind his ear
that felt so good
Sutter tilted his head to one side
to make sure I got it
just the way he liked
then he limped back to his wagon
and Mr. Portee

Lettie
Arkansas / June 1879

Daddy says we don't need
no one but ourselves
But today
when we weren't
but five miles out of our camp
our wagon wheel
got stuck so deep in a rut
Charly or Titus couldn't make it move
not even an inch
even after we took out
our chests and
all of our supplies

and laid them on the ground
to make it lighter to pull
Daddy ran ahead
then every single one of the men
stopped their wagons and came over
arguing about what was best
till they finally
filled the ruts with sandy soil
and laid down one of the blankets
we used for the horses
underneath the wheels
and pushed
and pulled
with everything they had
Elijah and Silas
clapped loud
when they heard the wagon wheels creaking

then rolling
inch by inch
out of the mud onto solid ground
Sweat was dripping like a river
down Daddy's face
The men smacked each other's backs
They helped us put everything
back in our wagon
and we started again
on our way
Safer in numbers

Lettie
Arkansas / June 1879

Why we stopping?
Silas asked

as all the wagons
slowed
The road we were on
was so bendy
I could barely see what was ahead
but as I stepped out in front
around the curve in the road
I could see another company up ahead
but they weren't all colored
like us
with ten wagons
they were smaller
all one family it looked like
and white
The road
was hardly big enough for one
so we kept apart
best as we could
Them coming one way
us going the other
until the white company
stopped altogether
and two of their men
got down and came over

to Mr. Casey's wagon
I was standing beside Charly
and I waved away the flies
over his back

Daddy got down
off the wagon seat
and Momma
came around next to him
and put her hand
on his arm
holding him back
or pushing him forward
I couldn't tell
But Daddy stood still
and quiet for once
just listening
to words no one
but Mr. Casey could hear
They didn't talk for long
and when their wagons left
and went past us
I waved
Hello
and *goodbye*
Mr. Casey called us over
That there was the Pennington family
They coming from
where we going to

Mr. Portee asked
They leaving Nebraska?
Sutter was sitting by his side
in the wagon seat
I walked over
and reached up
to Sutter
I held out my hand
Sutter set his paw
warm and scratchy
on top of my hand
Smart boy Sutter
I whispered
so Daddy didn't hear

Said there was tough going
after Independence
Some of the companies
had some problems with bandits
up that way

You talking Indians?
Mr. Anderson asked
holding his wife Odette close

Nah
He didn't say nothing about Indians
What I hear
they ain't been known to give any trouble
lest you go asking
Matter of fact
I'm counting on their help
if we can find it
I'd like to speak with the men tonight
over at my wagon
Let's not lose any more of our day

I don't know how many more days are ahead
but Daddy told me to stop thinking about
hours and days
and more about
weeks and months
It was too hard
to keep the miles in my head
so I started writing them down
in the supply book
I kept for Momma and Daddy
along with other things
I had a mind to write down
that got nothing to do with numbers
things I've been noticing
but keep to myself
like the way Momma and Daddy
don't talk like they used to
and Momma is so tired
all the time
she needs my help with nearly all the cooking
and cleaning up
and watching Silas and 'lijah

The way Daddy talks
about the other families
and how we don't need them
They uppity
They think they better

Momma says
his words aren't *Christian talk*
But mostly
I've been noticing how
the quiet of Momma and Daddy
makes me feel an alone
I never felt at home
and we still got
weeks and months
to go

Sylvia
Arkansas and crossing into Missouri / June 1879

I see Lettie
writing in the book
I gave her
There's not much Lettie don't see
she takes in the world around her
breathes it in deep
like her daddy I suppose
Each day
a chance to see
feel
live
more than the one before
There are times
it is hard to see the beauty
my Lettie sees
wildflowers coming to bloom
birds sending us greetings
all along the way
mile after blessed mile
walking mostly
till I can't feel my legs

I watch her watching
me and Thomas
Elijah and Silas
and all the others
noticing what most don't care to
adding it up maybe
like the numbers she keeps
for our supplies
hoping it makes sense
She sees me tired
and dragging most days
but her figuring
and watching
and writing in her book
is never going to tell her
what's so plain to any woman
but not to Lettie's eyes yet
a child still
that by the time our wagon
pulls into our homestead in Nebraska
there won't be no hiding
the baby
I'm carrying inside me

Lettie
Missouri / June 1879

They said you a baby
too young to come
exploring with us

I heard Elijah
telling Silas
Momma had me gathering
sticks
for the supper fire later
I didn't mind
It was the only time
the whole day long
I didn't have to mind
my brothers
and could go off
with my book

under a tree with nobody asking
What you writing Lettie?
and
Let me see
But even by myself
I could still hear them
and see Silas
from where I was sitting

No I'm not
Silas said to Elijah

I could hear him already
at the edge of crying

You is too a baby
You already crying
Elijah laughed
leaving him behind
alone

'lijah!
Silas yelled
running to keep up
I got up
put my book and pencil back in my pocket
and walked over

Don't pay him no mind
I told Silas

but he kept up his running
Elijah never looked back
laughing as he ran alongside
Presley and Duke
Laughing just like they laughed
loud
mean
and nothing like
Elijah

Silas
Come on back here
I yelled to him

68

You wanna help me
go hunting for sticks?

With Silas
as long as I said *hunting*
he'd do most anything
Hunting for firewood
Hunting for water
Hunting for berries
But this time I said it
Silas stayed looking
where Elijah left off running
put his hands in his pockets
and sat down hard in the grass
tearing it out
in clumps
I held out my hand to him

You ready to go hunting?

but Silas pushed my hand away
and took off
running just like Elijah had
But he ran off
into the trees

Silas!
I shouted now to his back
I can't come after you
Come on back here!

Momma came out from behind the wagon
Who you shouting at girl?
she said wiping her hands
on the skirt of her dress

Silas ran off
I told her

He fine
he's with his brother

Elijah's not with him
He went with the Lorton boys

Momma made a face
He'll come on back
when he's hungry
You get those sticks for the fire?

Getting them now Momma
I looked all around
but Silas was gone

Sylvia
Missouri / June 1879

When dark came on
and Silas
wasn't nowhere to be found
I had to go and tell Thomas
what Lettie told me
He didn't pay me no mind at first

They just being boys
Go on and tell Lettie
to look for them around camp
and bring 'em on back for supper
he said
tending to the wagon wheel he was fixing

But when I told him
that Elijah been back at camp
an hour now
and hadn't seen his brother
fact is
no one had seen Silas
since he ran off
He dropped his tools where he stood
and took off toward Elijah
Thomas is not one
to hide his temper
If I can say one thing for him
his own children
never been on the end of it
but when he tore out after Elijah
I knew that was about to change

Before I could catch him
he snatched Elijah's arm

How'd you leave your brother?
he screamed

Thomas don't . . .
I told him

But he shook me off
Elijah fell out crying
Thomas shoved him down
screamed some more

He's your brother—

I could hear the words
choking
in his voice

*You got to look out
for your own
Don't you never forget that*

Thomas went to the wagon
grabbed his hat
a lantern
his gun
unhitched Charly from the wagon
Folks stopped what they were doing
started walking over

Silas!
Thomas shouted
Anyone seen my boy?
Silas!

He turned to the folks
coming to our camp
They were shaking their heads
No
He jumped on Charly
and started out

The Caseys
took out after him
Jackson Lorton too
and the Cole brothers and Tom Portee
and all I could hear
was the sound of hooves
and men running
and calling
for my Silas
and Thomas's yelling
growing softer
and softer
Where is my boy?

Lettie
Missouri / June 1879

Me and Momma
shouted till Silas's name
came out in whispers
Silas!
Silas!
over and again
but no one could find him
It was like the woods
had gone
and swallowed him up
for its supper
Elijah couldn't move
from the log by the fire
where he sat
crying so hard
he could barely breathe
As much as I wanted to be mad
for him leaving Silas behind
for making him run off
every time I looked at his face
I wanted to cry
right along with him
Presley and Duke
knew better than to show
their faces near our camp
but their daddy was out with ours

hunting the woods
for Silas
Hunting
Was Silas out hunting now for something?
Or was he lost
and scared
and just
hunting for us?

Lettie
Missouri / June 1879

In the morning
Momma fried bacon
and made coffee
for breakfast
Elijah sat so close to Silas
he was about on his lap

Give the boy room
Daddy yelled at Elijah
He ain't 'bout to go
get hisself lost again
Is you Silas?

Silas shook his head no
at Daddy
Elijah moved over
to give Silas room
but not nearly enough
Silas smiled over at him
his big smile
I could tell
wanting Elijah
to stay right where he was
next to him

Daddy said he found Silas
hiding underneath
an old rotten tree trunk
scared to stay
too scared to come back

I saw a snake
he told Daddy
This long
He held his hands out
as wide as his arms could stretch
So I hid

Mr. Casey told Silas
That was smart

And Mr. Portee laughed
and said
I would have done the exact same thing

Daddy told Silas
Me
I ain't never liked no snakes
but you gave us all a scare Silas
We thought we lost you
and on the way back
Silas asked Daddy
Am I a baby?

You my baby boy
and that's what you always gonna be
Grown or no
Daddy said he told him
that don't make you less
Anybody say different
you tell them
come and see me

Where the biscuits?
Daddy yelled at Momma

Seemed all Daddy could do now
was yell
Momma looked up at him
from her eating
like she was figuring out an answer
to something
she already knew the answer to
I told you Thomas
She said so slow

she sounded sleepy
we nearly out of flour

Daddy took a big swallow of his coffee
Took another bite of his bacon
That my fault?
he asked Momma

*Not looking to find fault
just stating facts Thomas*

Facts?
Daddy said
*Well fact is
we'll stock up when we get to Independence*

How far is Independence Daddy?
I asked
*Say about another week or two
we be there
You can do without biscuits till then
can't you Lettie?*
Daddy smiled

I smiled back
smiled at Momma too
Sure can

We can too
shouted 'lijah and Silas
back sitting
right on top of each other
Only one not smiling
was Momma

75

Sylvia
Missouri / June 1879

Me and Clara
Dottie and her baby girl
sat together
while the men went out hunting
there was some deer

roaming the fields we walked
families
just like our ours
traveling as one
or stopping still
frozen scared as we passed
Their big eyes
watching
till we moved on
and they were safe again
but mostly
there were plenty
of groundhogs
too fat
to move fast

We gonna be eating good tonight
Thomas told me this morning
loading his rifle
He was the first one
to raise his hand
to volunteer
when they got up a hunting party

What we get
we'll split between us all
fair and even

Never mind
he'd be lucky to get one
seeing as he wasn't
no hunting man
But I was hoping
someone
the brothers
Hark and Oscar Cole
Mr. Portee maybe
would

They all
Dottie said
lived on what they hunted

Not like the rest of us
Farmers
who grew
and slaughtered
traded
every so often and bought
when we needed
I thought Thomas could even learn
if he watched
did more listening
than talking
I asked Lettie to take the boys
berry hunting
Wasn't so much needing berries
as much as I was needing
time with Dottie and Clara
to make some part of me
whole again
Every day we travel
the hurt of leaving Olivia
and my brothers
felt like leaving pieces of me
along the trail
I worry by the time we reach Nebraska
there won't be much left

William says
little more than a week
to Independence
Clara told us
Sure be nice to see some other folks
Not that I mind y'all's company

She laughed in a way
put me in the mind of my sister
with her pretty white teeth
Her husband William got family
already waiting for them in North Platte

Heard Independence
is a right big city
Dottie said

Well we gonna stock up on supplies
We running low on nearly everything
I told them

Already?
Clara asked covering her mouth
and Dottie looked over at her
I'm sorry . . .

Just that we're barely starting out Sylvia
You can't be running out already?
Dottie said

Clara just means
you gonna pay more at the fort for everything

We got enough to share
Dottie said slowly
If you need . . .

I shook my head
No
my pride
turning me away
from their kindness
or charity
I wasn't sure which
We went back to our sewing
I started humming
one of my favorite hymns
We are climbing Jacob's ladder . . .
Clara joined in
then Dottie
. . . Jacob's ladder . . .
that's when
we heard the screaming

Lettie
Missouri / June 1879

I was out
searching for mulberry bushes
Momma said she could at least

use the leaves
for tea
for healing
The season was early still
but I was hoping to find berries too
ripe enough already
to pick
Elijah and Silas
were dragging along behind
not looking at all
like I told them to
when we heard a shot first
the screaming second

What's that?
shouted 'lijah
looking up from his worm digging
I stood
covering my eyes from the sun
Looking out into the woods
where my daddy
and the men
went hunting for deer
Sutter too
leading the way with Mr. Portee
one ear up
listening
his nose to the ground
I was betting he was once
a good hunting dog
when he was younger
and faster
I didn't see nothing but trees
and then I saw some of the men
running out from the woods
They were holding up
one man
with blood
running everywhere
his face
his chest
his hands
dripping onto the men carrying him
So much

I couldn't make out
who he even was
But I knew it wasn't my daddy
because Daddy was running behind
his rifle waving wild
in the air
I was afraid
he was gonna shoot us
with all his waving
Hurry!
I yelled to my brothers
and for the first time ever
they minded me
we ran toward the men
but they were running so fast
we couldn't catch up

Sylvia
Missouri / June 1879

At first
we couldn't tell who was hurt
Hark and Oscar came running
carrying one other in their arms
all of them covered in blood
The others came up
a few minutes later
It was Butch Anderson
hurt bad
Go and get Odette
someone shouted

Don't know who did
but just like that
she come running
How? How?
shouting at the men

Shot hisself
Jackson Lorton said
Grabbed the muzzle
Next thing we knew—

He never done much hunting
Odette said

She knelt down to him
wiped his blood
with the hem of her dress

Where's the blood coming from?
she screamed
to Butch
everyone
But no one knew
took us all
to strip him down
find the hole where the bullet went in
and out

Clean at least
Amos said

Staring down at Butch
Dottie had some nurse training
so I held her baby
while she yelled over her shoulder
Heat some water
set a knife in the fire
wet some cloths

We all ran every which way
while Butch lay still in the dirt
silent
Odette holding his hand
and staring in his eyes
just like she always did

Lettie
Missouri / June 1879

I covered
Elijah and Silas's eyes
once we reached the men
hid them behind me

while I watched my momma and Miss Dottie
tend to Mr. Anderson
in the dirt
Miss Clara brought over a blanket
Daddy came over
knelt down to us
Take your brothers back to the wagon
he told me
You don't want to see this here

But what happened?
I asked him

Accident
is all he would say

Elijah looked to me
Lettie . . .
tears running now

Shhh shhh
I told him

and then Silas started
with his one question more

Is he gonna die?

I held their hands
walking them back
and shushing them both
trying to stop their crying
and mine too

Sylvia
Missouri / June 1879

Just need to make sure
infection don't set in
Dottie said
after Butch was bandaged and resting
Odette setting beside him

That night
lying next to Thomas
I thought of Odette
holding Butch's hand
and lay thinking

Who is going to drive their team now
with him laid up
and his new wife waiting to see
if he was going to live
or die?
I thought too
about making my way
West
without Thomas by my side
hard as it was
It'd be harder still
on my own
I reached for Thomas's hand
in the dark

Be careful
I said to him

You ain't got to worry 'bout me
he said
a laugh in his voice
I know how to shoot a gun
without shooting myself

Lettie
Missouri / July 1879

That night
after Elijah and Silas
were asleep
and Silas asked more questions
than Momma wanted to answer
about hunting
about Butch Anderson
about if he was going to die
Momma called me to the fire

Sit with me
she said
and held my hand
trying I could tell
to keep me from asking more of the same questions
my brothers did
Dottie got her nurse training
in the war
helping to treat
soldiers from the North
and anyone fighting with them
That's how she met William
Momma told me
smiling
He run off
from the man
who owned him
back in Tennessee
made his way
down to fight with those Union boys
and got himself hurt bad
Was Dottie that was there with him
when he woke up
Held his hand at night
when he was crying out
William told her
I make it through
You better get yourself ready
to keep on holding my hand
Dottie didn't pay him no mind
seeing as she was just doing her job
But soon as the war ended
He came back
found her
and made her
his wife
We lucky to have Dottie with us
She's taking good care
of Mr. Anderson
just like she did with William
and Butch and Odette
are going to be able
to make a life together
in Nebraska

just like they planned
We best get ready for bed
Momma patted my hand
like I seen Mrs. Anderson
pat her husband's

Mr. Casey's son Emmanuel
drove the Anderson wagon
because Mr. Anderson was still
too sick to drive it
He had to ride in back
with Mrs. Anderson
His fever wouldn't break
Momma said
no matter what Miss Dottie did
Odette is gonna stay on in Independence
and see to a doctor
till Butch is well enough
to travel again
maybe even turn back
If he isn't
Momma told me
But could he . . .

Now hush with that talk Lettie
We gonna pray the good Lord spares him
Momma answered me back
before I could finish
That didn't mean we could wait
We'd have to keep on
leaving them further behind
or get further behind ourselves
Just like that
we're gone from ten families
to nine

Lettie
Missouri / July 1879

It seemed
no matter how tired we were
all us families
found time to get together

at night
around a fire every now and again
There was talking
and telling stories
of who
and what
they left behind
and what they hoped for
ahead
My daddy
did a lot of talking then
about the land
he was going
to farm
and everyone nodded
their heads
saying
they heard
the planting
may be hard
but with strong hands
and hard work
it could be done

Well
I surely got strong hands
Daddy would tell them
holding his hands out
for everyone to see
Momma
would rub Daddy's back
I think
making sure
his voice didn't get too loud
like it sometimes did
when he got to talking about
Dreams
Everybody had them
all different in some way
but the same too
wanting more than they had
and more than they'd ever seen
Not one knowing
what the West was like

but trusting
that with God
it was gonna be better
than what they were leaving
behind
Because if it wasn't
then all these miles we walked
was for nothing
and they'd be the fools
in the end
No one said that part
out loud
They didn't have to
but I could hear it

As much as I liked the stories
of families back home
and dreams
I liked the music
singing
and dancing more
Miss Dottie's husband
Mr. Baker
brought out his fiddle
that he sometimes strummed with a bow
Sometimes plucked with his fingers
till we clapped along
and it was almost always
Miss Arlene
the quietest
of the three Boston sisters
who sang
The other two
Miss Ellen and Miss Heloise
just about begging
C'mon Arlene
sing that song we like
until finally she would
with her eyes closed
and her hands behind her back
Her voice was happy
and sad
at the same time
Momma told me later

her sisters made her sing
so that their momma
lying back in the wagon
with their daddy watching over her
could hear
Music heals
Momma told me
I hoped it would heal
Mr. Anderson too
back in his wagon with his wife

When Mr. Baker played fast
he'd sing songs with his deep deep voice
that could make you dance
Mr. Oscar would stand up
and start flapping his arms
and grab someone
anyone
he didn't much care who
to dance with him
His brother Hark
The other Mr. Cole
would shout
Sit down you old fool
but he was clapping
and laughing along too
Once Momma
pulled at Daddy's hands
trying to get him to get up
and dance with her
but he waved her hands away
stayed sitting
and staring into the fire
Elijah and Silas yelled

Dance Daddy

and he looked over
at them
and I said too
Dance with Momma Daddy

Finally he stood
His feet
seemed heavy
his arms too
like they weren't even his
but holding Momma
and moving together
in time to the music
his feet and arms got lighter
Momma's head fell back
and along with our clapping
she laughed big
like she hadn't
in a long long time
And Daddy kept holding on
Those were the best nights
watching everyone's face
in the firelight
smiling
clapping
making all of us
feel good enough to dance
Our tired feet
healed
like Momma said
Almost forgetting
we had to go back
to our tents
and wake up
before the sun rose in the morning
to walk miles
and miles
and miles
all over again

Sylvia
Independence, Missouri / July 1879

When Thomas reached for the tin
hiding under the chest
holding the rest of our money
All that was left
from what we sold

in Natchez
it was light as a feather
You going by yourself?
I asked Thomas
hoping he didn't hear
the scared in me
Knowing that what Dottie and Clara
told me about how what we paid
in Mississippi
wasn't nothing like what we were going to pay
in Independence
with shopkeepers just waiting
for travelers
coming through town
with supplies low
and nowhere else to turn
starting out
on any of the trails
and knowing they could charge them
nowhere nears what's right
or fitting
but as much as they could get
It could happen easy
Dottie and Clara told me
to someone
who didn't know their numbers or letters
or had a mind to buy whatever
he saw fit
someone
they didn't need to say
like my Thomas

Lettie

Independence, Missouri / July 1879

When our wagons
pulled into Independence
the town sounded to me
just like it felt
Like I heard how folks back home
talk about
when slavery days were over
and they had no more master
and everyone was independent

free
they said
to get up in the morning
when they wanted
without the call of the morning bell
free
to leave and go
where they wanted
without a pass

Us colored folks
ain't never gonna be free
the way white folks is
We gotta find
our own kind of free
Daddy told me

Independence looked to me
like colored folks may have found
their own kind of free
coming and going
to do just as they pleased

Seemed overnight
I went from hearing
sounds I knew
to ones I hadn't heard
in a long time
or not at all
I just about spun in circles
at first
till Daddy took my hand in his
and led me
down the street
There was
hammering at the blacksmith
carriages and wagons
not caring at all
who was in their way
and rushing past me
music and folks pouring drinks
coming from a store called a *Saloon*
Daddy hurried me past
telling me

Ain't nothing going on there
you need to see

but I looked in anyhow
When we passed a house
With a sign hanging out front
for a Doctor Barlow
I asked my daddy
Is that where
Mr. Anderson will go?

Maybe so baby girl
Daddy said
shaking his head
This morning
Mr. Anderson had stopped eating
But Mrs. Anderson
held tight to his hands
Praying and telling him
You gonna be just fine Butch
But I knew
they'd never catch up to us
on the trail now

Colored folks in Independence
were just like white folks
in Natchez
buying and selling
from their own stores and carts
Some looked as raggedy as we did
Others looked like they
would never have to move
miles from home
in a wagon
with everything they owned
because they already had
all they could ever want
right here
It seemed like
no one looked afraid
to speak their mind
no one needed to bow their heads
or step aside
because a white person

was passing
Shops and carts on the square
sold everything
I could feel my mouth
full of water
when we passed by the
apples
roasting meat
fresh bread
There were belts and medicines
furs and hides
shovels and combs
saddles and lace
I wanted all of it
but knew we didn't have
the room in our wagon
or the money in our tin
Momma told me to keep account of
Not just in my book neither
This is all we got Lettie
You best stay close to your daddy
make sure he comes back
with something in his pocket
she whispered away from Daddy
but I nearly forgot
what Momma said when we started out
I didn't know where to settle my eyes
and everywhere I looked
reminded me
how little we had
especially when I saw folks
dressed so fine
I looked down at my dusty dress
torn-up stockings
muddy
run-over boots

Why can't we live here?
I asked Daddy

This just our jump-off to the trail
Daddy said
pulling me along
We ain't come all this way

to stay packed together
like cattle in a pen
Where we going
we gonna have land

He stretched his hands
out in front of him

Peace and quiet
not like this
We gonna build our own
from the ground up
without folks coming round
putting their noses in our business

Daddy nodded to me
then to hisself
But it seemed
that being near people
even if they weren't family
wasn't so bad
because all the new folks
we met in our company
Mr. Portee and Sutter
The Cole brothers
Miss Clara
and the Lortons
Miss Dottie and her baby girl
sweet almost as Vivvy was what was making
our wagon trip
traveling day in
and day out
together
feel like home

Sylvia
Independence, Missouri / July 1879

I first saw her talking
with Marshall Day
She was vexed I could see
Marshall was looking over her shoulders
to her left and right

like he had someplace else
he needed to be
Next it was Oscar
she was talking with
and his head was shaking back and forth
No
I made my way over to Clara's wagon

Who's she?
I asked pointing to the woman

Most likely trying to join up
get West somewheres
We stood together
staring
watching

Where's her people?

Clara laughed then
You ask more questions
than I know what to do with
I went back to our wagon
wondering
about the young woman
trying to get West
alone
without the safety
and company
of kin
now begging men with so many plans
freedoms
for their own selves
They didn't have time to study on
someone else's

Lettie
Independence, Missouri / July 1879

I walked beside Daddy
through the streets
packed so shoulder to shoulder
with folks

I could barely hear Daddy above the shouting
Finest saddles in town!
Best prices right here!
We passed a house called
a *Hotel*

Folks pay to sleep there
Daddy told me
and one sturdy stone house
that was a *Jail*
Daddy didn't need to tell me
who slept there
The marshal
stood outside
His arms were hugging his chest
looking like
if we stopped too long
we'd end up inside too
One store made newspapers
called the *Independent*
It had been so long
since I read any words
other than the ones
Momma had me read
sometimes at night
from the Bible
to Silas and Elijah
before bed
I was starting to miss school
of course Oda too
We always pretended
I was a teacher
when we made our schoolhouse
outside in back of her house
She was the student
and I taught her letters
and numbers
and Oda would raise her hand high
and say

You are the best teacher
I ever had Miss Lettie
And I'd say

Well you are the smartest student
I ever had Oda

and we'd laugh
I wanted so bad to read that *Independent* newspaper
and news of anyone
who lived in a town
louder than night sounds

Philomena
Independence, Missouri / July 1879

I was going to find my way to Nebraska
somehow
I had a job waiting on me
my very first
Teaching
in a small schoolhouse
in the town of
North Platte
I'd never been
that far West
The only towns
In Nebraska
I knew the names of
were Lincoln
and Omaha
But I knew
with the railroads
towns
were growing
bigger every day
with good jobs
and free land
for coloreds

Fact is
I'd never stepped
one foot
outside of Independence
but now
traveling West

to teach
gave me just the reason
I needed

But the only thing between me
and my new job
was getting there
When the school wrote

DEAR MISS PRATT,
THANK YOU FOR YOUR RECENT INQUIRY
WE ARE INDEED IN NEED OF A TEACHER WITH YOUR
QUALIFICATIONS
TO TEACH PRIMARY STUDENTS IN OUR AREA
THE SCHOOLHOUSE IS A NEW ONE
FUNDED BY THE RESOURCES OF OUR SMALL COMMUNITY
WE CAN ONLY OFFER
A SMALL COMPENSATION AND LODGING
WE DO HOPE THAT WILL SUFFICE . . .

I didn't need to read on
I knew I would take any position offered
if it got me far from Independence

Aunt Perlie and Uncle Edmund
could see
I was tickled
but had to ask one night at supper

How exactly do you plan on finding the fare?
You know we don't have it to give
After all we've done
for you
and your sister already
We couldn't possibly do more . . .

My aunt mumbled
the last part
under her breath
but her meaning was clear
No more *charity* from them

What about your savings?
my uncle offered

I have some Uncle Edmund
but the train fare
is much more than I thought it would be
I told him
If I use my savings on the fare
I'm not sure I'll have enough left over
to set myself up once I arrive
The pay is quite low . . .

They went back to eating
leaving me
to find my own answers

Lettie
Independence, Missouri / July 1879

How could one place
smell like so many things
all at once?
Fire and smoke
wood and coal from a forge

hot yeasty bread
at the bakers
Manure from horse stalls
Mud
from everywhere
Daddy wasn't taking time
to see it all like I was
He was rushing me
to the grocery and supply store
in the middle of town
Momma had me write down what she needed
flour
salt
five pounds of bacon
cornmeal
a little coffee
and if I could find them
some eggs
just because
we need a little something special
she told me

and I wanted to
find them
just to see her smile
and see what she could make
special
on the trail
when just cooking breakfast
took so long
and was so hard
some mornings
it hardly seemed worth it

Lettie
Independence, Missouri / July 1879

The General Store was the biggest I'd seen
with rows of things to buy
instead of just shelves
like the store we had
back home
There were
barrels in the front
for nails
beans
and molasses
Cans and cans of food
jars filled with candy on the counter
that Silas would have snatched
and eaten up
before I could have stopped him
I watched Daddy gather up what we needed
and when he stopped
to eye boots for himself
shiny and new
I found bolts of fabric
that looked the same
as the flowers I picked along the trail
purple and yellow
lavender, butterweed, and thistle
I knew Momma would have
made herself something
real pretty with that cloth

Something special
I remembered then
the eggs
remembered
if we bought
flower cloth for Momma
and shiny new boots for Daddy
and candy for Elijah and Silas
we'd likely starve before we got
West
I pulled Daddy along now
to pay for *just what we needed*
nothing more
like Momma told me
so we could bring something
to put back in the tin
But when we got to the counter to pay
and Daddy saw me looking past the jars of candy
to the stack of newspapers
on the floor
he reached down
put one copy of
the *Independent*
right along with our things
smiled big down at me
and I didn't say a word

Sylvia
Independence, Missouri / July 1879

It was nearly dark
time Thomas and Lettie got back
I had supper ready

Lettie's cheeks
looked like she's run back
mostway
to tell me all she saw
The streets running over
with people she said
the stores filled with so many pretty things . . .

You wouldn't believe it Momma

Any money left over?
I asked her

Yes she nodded
Told me how much
she counted went back in Thomas's pocket

Not more than a few coins
but it was something

You wrote everything down?
I asked her
and she patted the book
in her pocket
I turned to get their plates

Where's your daddy?
Lettie pointed behind her

*Daddy stopped to talk
to that woman*

And there she was
the woman from earlier
talking now to Thomas
I could see him laughing
his foot kicking dust in the dirt
not listening
hungry probably
aching to fill his belly

Stay with your brothers
I told Lettie
rushing over to Thomas
and the woman

Evening
She turned

Younger than I thought
I took her in
plain faced

proud
tall
strong

I'm Sylvia

Pleasure to meet you Miss Sylvia
My name is Philomena she told me
Philomena Pratt
She held out her hand to me to shake
like a man
I took it in mine
feeling its hardness
healed-over scabs
I looked into her eyes
· trying to make a match
between her well-spoken ways
and her hardworking hands

Thomas looked between the two of us

I'm Thomas's wife
I kept on
knowing he hadn't bothered with his name

A pleasure she said
I turned now to Thomas
Your supper is ready

Philomena
Independence, Missouri / July 1879

She was the only kind face I'd seen all day
Took the time to ask after me
my people
She wondered why I'd be traveling to Nebraska
all alone

I just finished my schooling
and I have a job there waiting
I figured if I join a company
like yours
I could earn my keep

cooking
cleaning
I worked as a laundress
to pay room and board
One thing I learned
living with my aunt Perlie and uncle Edmund
Is how to work
I told Miss Sylvia

She nodded
smiled
But she said what everyone else had that day
in every company I asked
We already tight
We just don't have the room
A woman traveling alone just isn't . . .

I tried once more
knowing
there weren't any more to turn to
with the late hour
the companies moving out first thing
my job starting soon
As she wished me well
bid me good night
I nearly shouted
I have money

Sylvia
Independence, Missouri / June 1879

Lord knows I needed the help
Lettie is doing all she can
to see to Elijah and Silas
Thomas is out
seems every day now
hunting and fishing
with the men
but most times
coming back
with berries and plants
With just the coins left in our tin

and our chest still with not enough supplies
to get us to Nebraska
like Philomena
we'll be needing the charity of those
in our company
to see us through
Tired as I am
I could use Philomena's help
with the cooking
laundry
It's clear to me
she's no stranger
to hard work
But when I got back to the wagon
I told Thomas
much as I could use her hands
our family could use her money more

Lettie
Independence, Missouri / July 1879

There were colored companies like ours
in wagons
Some just had tents
and you could smell cooking meat
over the fire
folks talking
laughing
a banjo
almost like a celebration
We were over fifty days from home
and here we were
in a place
that made me feel
the most like home
There were days
I was so tired
after walking
and chasing after my brothers
and helping Momma
with all she needed
I could barely remember

Oda
my aunt, uncles
and baby Vivvy's face
The tired
made the missing easier
But in Independence
when I looked at all the faces
I was expecting to see
someone I knew
from back home
I could almost feel
Oda's hand in mine
and hear Uncle Benton's
big laugh
and the hurting
started all over again

While Momma was talking
to a woman
I'd never seen
I got Elijah and Silas settled in
then laid down a blanket
Folks had finally started getting their camps
ready for the night
I heard someone singing to their baby
I stared up at the sky
thinking how I'd miss this town
partway
between my old home
and my new one
I listened for the owls and crickets
but all I heard
was the sound of a train whistle

Philomena
Independence, Missouri / July 1879

Miss Sylvia told me her girl Lettie
was bright
Sharper than I know what to do with
she said
So when I hurried back home
and was packing my things
I brought along a speller

and two extra books
in my small bag
thinking it'd be good practice for my teaching

When I said goodbye
to Aunt Perlie
and Uncle Edmund
my aunt told me I best be on the lookout
for a husband
Soon as you can
so's you have someone to take care of you
I nodded
and kissed them goodbye
thanking them for all they've done
since my own momma and daddy passed
long ago now of the fever
when I was just barely past five
But Aunt Perlie didn't know
I had no plan
on leaving their home
where every word
was questioned
every decision
was judged
A home where
I was reminded daily
of their *obligation*
just to find a husband
and do it all over again

Sylvia
Independence, Missouri / July 1879

We left Independence
on the Sabbath
A pastor in town
came over to the campsite
to give the word to all those traveling

In the Book of Exodus
Moses led his people
out of Egypt
to the Promised Land . . .

Some folks stood
others were on their knees
in the mud
Go forth!
The pastor shouted
his hands holding his Bible
over his head
I felt my own hands lifting
high
higher
above my head
to the heavens
and closed my eyes
Together
we all rejoiced
in song
and prayer
my faith restored
Go forth
into the Promised Land

Church on the trail
wasn't the same as sitting in a pew
in Benton's church
but it felt good just the same

After service
I passed women sitting together
working together
gathering up
their pots and pans
trunks
their children
for the next part
of their journeys
Some were leaving out
on the Santa Fe Trail
others on the California Trail
but all of us
were heading West
far from here
and farther from where we started
They finished
watering their animals

just like us
before our next stretch
of travel
Thomas was aching to get on

. . . lost half the day worshipping
when we need to be walking

he was saying to himself
when I got back to the wagon

Lettie
Independence, Missouri / July 1879

I didn't understand when Momma told us
that morning
at breakfast
we were taking a passenger
with us to Nebraska
the woman I saw her talking to

Miss Philomena Pratt
She's going to help us till we get to Nebraska
She'll only travel with us partway
just till we get
to what will be our new home
in Kearney
and then she'll have to travel on
maybe with another family
I'll see if Clara
or Dottie
can find room to take her on
to her teaching job
farther West in North Platte

Suppose they don't want to take her?
Elijah asked
What's she gonna do then?

Well I don't know Elijah
There is a train—

Where she gonna sleep?
Silas asked

We'll make do
Momma said
We may have to leave a few things behind
to make room for Miss Pratt
But I'll be glad for her help

Daddy kept right on chewing
not saying a word to any of Momma's

Are her momma and daddy coming too?
Silas asked

And this one time
I was glad to have brothers
who asked all the questions I wanted to
but knew Momma would say wasn't fitting
for a young girl
to be questioning things she ought not be

But what my brothers didn't ask
was the one thing I wanted to know most
If we barely had enough for us
How are we ever
going to have enough
for someone else?

PART THREE

· · · · · · · · · · · · · · · ·

I had no idea
how my story would unfold
out West
But I knew one thing
it was finally
my story to write
any way I saw fit
—Philomena

Philomena
Independence, Missouri / July 1879

After my one bag
was loaded onto the Grier family wagon
I met Lettie, Elijah, and the little one
Silas
scarce as they were
I barely saw them
but I could tell
those boys would be a handful
Miss Sylvia told me that Lettie
had reached her eleventh year
shortly before they left
Are you a teacher?
Lettie asked me right off
I couldn't quite tell from her asking
what answer she wanted

She introduced me to Charly and Titus
They're easy to tell apart
She pointed
Charly is the handsome one
with the white spot above his ear
She laid her head on his nose
and he loves to be kissed right here
The mule grunted
but Titus doesn't like that at all
Charly
Titus
I needed a ride to Nebraska
not a romance
with mules

Sylvia
Independence, Missouri / July 1879

Thomas was quiet
when I told the children
about Miss Pratt
He chewed slow

when I talked about how much of a help
she'd be
That morning
before she placed her one bag
on the wagon with ours
he reached out his hand to her
open wide
and she handed him over the bills
she promised to Thomas
He counted them in front of her
making sure she knew
he didn't trust her kind
a young woman
on her own
not seeming to need no help
from a man
Thomas knows better
but acts like he doesn't sometimes
But I kept my tongue

When we set off
walking side by side
I watched her face
out the corner of my eye
to see if I saw in her
any of what I felt
leaving Natchez behind
She chatted polite
pointed to the people she knew from town
the stores she visited
where she worked as a laundress
But not once
did she look like she was leaving behind
anything
anyone
she'd miss
and not once
like me
did she look back

Lettie
Missouri / July 1879

Outside of Independence
we passed small cabins lined up neat
along the road
sometimes folks came out
and waved
or just stared as we passed

When we stopped
Mr. Spruill let me trace his trail map
with my finger
This here
He put a circle around a spot
with his chewed-down pencil
pointing to a crooked line on the map
This is where we got to cross
the Kansas River
The Kaw
some folks call it
he laughed
sounding like the crows
we heard
up in the trees
as we walked

Are we getting another flatboat
to get us all across?
I asked him

Not this time Lettie
There's no boats anywhere nearby
that can take us
'sides
thinking we can get across
this time
without one

You mean
We're all gonna swim?
I asked him
Mr. Spruill laughed some more

Well now, most folks can't
me especially
Mr. Spruill's laugh
was as loud as Uncle Benton's
So the plan is
we run a rope across
He put one finger on one side of the crooked line
another finger on the other
All we got to do is hold on
and walk across

He folded up his map
and put it in his pocket
smiled at me kind
You can do that can't you sweetheart?

Lettie
Missouri / July 1879

There were more wagons
out on the trail today
more than we'd seen before
But all spread out
far enough so you couldn't see
who folks were
or talk if you wanted to

Momma was too tired today to walk far
so after she laid down in the wagon
and Silas chased off after Elijah
I walked next to Miss Pratt
Your momma says you love your lessons

I do ma'am
I told her
not mentioning that
even though I could keep an accounting
of our books to add up
how much supplies cost
I didn't like arithmetic nearly as much
as I did writing
I didn't think she'd want to hear that

Have you enjoyed your journey so far?
she asked me
I could tell she was trying to be kind
And even though I knew we had already walked
fifty days or more
and almost 700 miles
We still have about another 450 miles to go.
I didn't want to talk to Miss Pratt about traveling
as much as I wanted to ask her
Are you scared to go West?
Do you think you'll like being a teacher?
Where are your momma and daddy?
She looked too young to be a teacher
but old enough
that I wanted to ask
Shouldn't you have a husband?

Sylvia
Missouri / July 1879

Thomas didn't like us
taking on a stranger

We don't know her people

He kept up with his mumbling
even after Philomena gave him money
for her passage

And she best not cause
one bit of trouble
or I'm putting her out

He wasn't going to do no such a thing
I know he wasn't proud to be needing
her money
He'd likely tell the others
He *felt sorry for her*
It was the Christian thing to do
seeing as she's all alone
he'd say
We had traveled so many miles
the last week

with not enough food in our bellies
and me carrying a child
is taking more out of me than I got
But I am getting most tired
of listening to Thomas
talk big
to cover how he's feeling
so small

Philomena
Missouri / July 1879

I was born
in April of 1861
the day the War Between the States began
my uncle Edmund once told me

Most likely
that's what made you a fighter
Shame before God
your momma
daddy
never got to see you grown

If being a fighter
is what made me live on
after the fever took
my momma and daddy

and last year
my sister Phoebe too
I'm not so sure
there was much use in it
Was I fighting to live
to be free
get an education
just to be
all by myself?
It's as if I were born
knowing how to work
Aunt Perlie saw it in me
and started me
almost as soon as I could walk

helping her in the kitchen
Mixing batter first
Rolling dough second
Scrubbing pots
floors later
My mind needs busyness
Some call their cleaning time
mindless work
but I say it is the time
when your mind
is working hard
while your hands tend to the mindless
Soon as Aunt Perlie let me
I found paying work
doing much the same
The time I had away from her
and collecting coins for my trouble
was well worth it
Girls laughed
at my hands
spotted and scarred and scratched
The hands of
a fighter

While I am not currently interested
in marrying
I suppose I will one day
as is required
after I'm settled into teaching
and my new home
and have a chance to live on my own
West
I never knew what it was like
to have a momma and daddy
I can't even remember their faces
the sound of their voices
so I worry how I'm ever
going to one day
be a mother myself
Aunt Perlie had none of her own
and caring for me and Phoebe
wasn't something that came natural
It was her *Christian duty*
not family love
to care for us

and she reminded us
nearly every day

I imagine the kind of mother
I hope to be
want to be
when I look at Miss Sylvia
so patient
so proud of her boys and Lettie
But I haven't found a man
I can ever imagine being a wife to
especially
truth be told
if it was someone
like Sylvia's Thomas

Sylvia
Missouri and crossing into Kansas / July 1879

There are days
when it is easier
walking on tired feet
than trying to rest on blankets
in the back of our wagon
Today I felt the bones in my back
were near to breaking
with the bumping along
seems like we hit
every rock and branch
and Lord knows what else
I tried humming the hymns I sang
back home
to Lettie, Silas, and Elijah
Time this child comes
he won't know what it means
to sit still
There is a balm in Gilead
to make the wounded whole
There is a balm in Gilead
to heal the sin-sick soul
When the rains started
beating down on our wagon cover
is when I finally fell asleep

Lettie

Kansas / July 1879

The rains
just kept coming
and wouldn't stop
Elijah and Silas
kicked at the holes
filled with water
stomped in them

My dress
was so soaked through
and heavy
it felt like
I had on ten
The rain and mud
ran through the holes in my boots
but there wasn't enough room
in the wagon for all of us

and with Momma resting now
I knew not to wake her
just to keep dry
so I kept on
not even minding my steps
or our miles
not enough
to even bother counting
trying not to cry in front of Miss Pratt
and show her I was as strong
as Momma made me out to be
even with Elijah and Silas
making a muddy mess out of everything
Miss Pratt
walked and talked
like the sun was shining bright
as the rain poured down
near all day

Philomena

Kansas / July 1879

Lord it rained
so hard I was sure
there couldn't be no more rain
left in the clouds
Finally we had to stop
when the roads
nearly disappeared in front of us
and Mr. Casey's oxen refused to go farther
I could have kept on
knowing each step
was one more
away from Independence
and closer to Nebraska
I checked in on Miss Sylvia
lying on top of a pile of blankets in the wagon
She looked as worn out
as if she'd been walking
the miles we had
right alongside us all morning

Under the wide branches of a tree
I stripped off some dry bark
best as I could
and started a fire
made coffee
fried bacon
In the fat of the bacon left in the skillet
I made some corn cakes
I had Lettie bring a plate to her momma
but she brought it back full

Momma said she doesn't have the stomach for it
just yet
maybe later

Thomas talked to his boys
and still not one word for me
We were all soaked through
I was thankful for the break from the rain
and a chance to rest my tired feet

but as thankful
as I wanted to be
for the warming fire
it wasn't nearly enough
to take away the coldness of Thomas

Philomena
Kansas / July 1879

What are you writing?
I asked Lettie

She sat in the corner of the wagon
with a small ledger in her lap
used for keeping numbers

She keeps an accounting of our numbers
and everything else she sees
Right Lettie?
Sylvia answered for her
She rubbed Lettie's back
Lettie looked up at me
and smiled shy
went right on back to her writing
The wagon was smaller
than I imagined it would be
even with both ends open
and a breeze blowing through
it still smelled
of wet clothes
smoke from the fire
sweat
coffee and dried meats
that were stored away
in one of the chests
It was sure warmer
and dryer
than walking outside
but no more pleasing
I reached in my bag
where I had the book I packed

Any interest in a story?
Silas covered his ears
and Elijah laughed at that

You'll have to pardon them
Seems being so far from home
made them forget their manners
Isn't that right Silas?
Elijah?

When Sylvia brought them both outside
I assume for a talking-to
Lettie looked at me

I like stories
she told me
and
She reached in the corner of the wagon
I have a newspaper

Lettie
Kansas / July 1879

I was somewhere between sleep
and wake
when I heard voices
I never heard before
loud
mean
deep voices
that didn't sound
nothing like the ones
in our company

White men?
When it was time for bed
I found a dry spot
under our wagon
and stared out at the moon
curved like a horseshoe tonight
I tried to count how many
tomorrows
on the trail we had left

Sixty?
Ninety?
Somewhere in between?
Daddy said it would be cold for sure
when we got there
Maybe too cold to start planting
so I wondered what we'd eat
and after I tossed all that around
in my head
I got wrapped up
good and warm
under my blankets
listening to the prairie dogs barking
and the coyote yelping
I just now was getting used to
It was a night
when no matter how hard I tried
I couldn't make my eyes stay open
for nothing
So I figured all that shouting
and fighting must be a dream
that came to me
because of my worrying

so I curled up
hugging myself tighter
hoping the dreams
filled with noise would stop
until I felt my arms being pulled
Lettie!
and Momma doing her best to whisper
Get in the wagon now!
through her crying
in the dark
Under the wagon where I was lying
all I could see
were shadows
of feet running this way
and that
Momma snatched me harder than she ever did
even when she was mad for my smart talking
I got up quick then
banging my head
on the underside
and ran behind Momma

up and into the wagon
where my brothers were already hiding
Miss Pratt's arms holding them
under blankets
Where's Daddy?
I asked
Momma covered my mouth with her hand
pointed to the front of the wagon
where all the noise was coming from
I wanted to see
and I didn't
So the five us sat quiet as we could
under the blankets
With just enough of the horseshoe moon
to see
You bleeding
Silas said
pointing to my head where I banged it

Shhh now
Momma put her finger to his lips
I wiped away blood
and we sat
waiting
for the fighting to stop
and the white men
to leave

Sylvia
Kansas / July 1879

Right after the war ended
and we were set free
we believed
all of us did
that couldn't nothing hurt us
the way master had
when we were slaves
Couldn't no one tell us
how to live
how to die
how to love
We thought freedom meant

125

we were free to do just as we pleased
safe
We thought that
right up until they came
late one night
banging hard on the front door of our cabin
shouting at my daddy
Open up!
My momma
stood behind my daddy
in her nightclothes
holding to him
My sister Olivia
went to get out of bed
told me

Shhh—
Stay here Syl—

Put her fingers to my lips
and walked quiet
so she could see
I walked behind
quieter
My brothers knew to stay put
My daddy already told them
what to do
but no one told us
thinking we were so young
we'd be too afeared to move
So when my momma
heard the floorboards creak
she ran to us
hoping we didn't see the men
who pushed open the door
to our cabin
shoved down our daddy
snatching at Momma
in her nightclothes
The men
shouting
white men words
But it was too late
Olivia saw and heard

and so did I
what happens at night
when sleep comes to us
but not to them
Just like tonight
when Thomas sat watch
in his job as Major
he took as serious
as if he were in a real army
giving everyone a shift
He always took the first one
the longest
He sat with two guns in his lap
One his own rifle
One pistol Beau let him hold
Thomas held those two guns
like he was waiting for trouble
He knew
just like I knew
trouble comes anytime
but especially at night

Lettie

Kansas / July 1879

I don't know how long we waited
Silas fell asleep
in Miss Pratt's arms
but Elijah kept his eyes open
wide
watching Silas sleeping
watching me resting my head
on Momma's shoulder
watching Momma sitting up straight
quieter than I ever seen him
The shooting outside
was making him remember
I think
Mr. Anderson
all the blood
the screaming
how bad he was hurt by his own gun
We didn't know

whose guns were shooting tonight
didn't want to
we just wanted to see Daddy
not get hurt
like Mr. Anderson

Philomena
Kansas / July 1879

I am trying
as best as I can
to commit to memory
what I don't want to forget
the horror of the evening
the fear of it
what Uncle Edmund warned me about
before I departed
Don't know what you gonna find
along those trails
he told me
Best keep your wits about you
your money close
Ain't no law out on the trail
Out there
folks
Godless men
live by their own rules
But more important than his words
was what he taught me
as I was growing into a young woman
He taught me
how to hold his Colt pistol
Like you shaking a hand
he told me
Phoebe never took to it
My aunt Perlie neither
but me and my uncle would go out
shooting some Saturdays
him with his rifle
me practicing
shooting rabbits
using all he taught me
So when I heard the shots come

128

in the middle of the night
I wished then I still had my uncle's pistol
by my side
I knew right away
what he told me was true
that some folks
think they got a right to what's yours
That in a land with no laws
the person who's the best shot
gets to keep what's theirs
I knew Thomas had been keeping first watch
I knew it was the only job
they'd give him
the lowliest
but I could see his pride in it
I heard him tell Miss Sylvia one night
as he left for his watch

They all thinking
they big men
leading
bossing folks
but there ain't gonna be no one to boss
someone come through
steal our mules
hurt our women
and children

I watched Miss Sylvia
rub his leg
nodding
soothing him I guess
So when the four men arrived
hoping
I heard
to make off with the mules
and teams of oxen
while everyone was sleeping
the way they do
Thomas was waiting
wide awake
He sent out a shot
and the others came running
But white men

thinking they owed something
don't run away that easy
so they stayed and fought
for animals
food
and anything else they thought they had a right to
Scared as I was
I was wishing
I could show everyone
all that Uncle Edmund taught me
with a pistol
But Thomas and the other men
did a good job
running them off
But only after one from our company
had been hurt
bad

Lettie
Kansas / July 1879

I held Momma's hand
as I watched Daddy
and the other men
shovel dirt over their shoulders

I listened in to the men talking
saying
they needed a hole
just deep enough
so the animals wouldn't come round
sniffing and digging

Back home
there was always a service
when someone passed on
food
singing
scripture from my uncle Benton
But here on the trail
there was just digging a hole
deep enough

and flowers
picked by some of the women
to lay down on top
Mr. Cole
the older of the brothers

dug harder
faster
than the others
and I saw
he had tears
running down his face
just as fast
as he was digging
I didn't much know Mr. Portee
but I liked him
and his dog
Sutter sat next to Mr. Portee
when he drove his wagon
small, and quiet
he had little pointy ears
just like Mr. Portee
I think he looked more like he was a brother to Mr. Portee
than his dog
if you ask me
Mr. Portee was the first to come
running with his gun
Daddy told me
when the men came
But one of the men
who came to steal
hit him hard in the head
and knocked him down
where he stood
Sutter was sitting now
next to their wagon
waiting I think
for Mr. Portee to get up
and come on back
give him his dinner scraps
but now just like Miss Pratt
he had no one
I asked Daddy if we could take him too

Only animal I aim to be caring for
is one working for me
Last I checked
that dog ain't doing nothing
but eating
and riding in a wagon
How's that helping me?

After the attack
Mrs. Lorton
who sometimes watched over my brothers
when they played with her boys
Presley and Duke
told her husband
if he didn't turn their wagon around
she'd take their children
and walk all the way back to Mississippi
without him

No telling what's coming next
she said loud enough for all of us to hear
Me and my children ain't going to die out here
in the middle of nowhere
like animals

Seems a shame to come all this way
just to turn right back around
But that's just what they did

Looked like they been following us all along
Daddy told me
Since we left Independence
need to be more careful
from here on

We lost time
and
and we had to hurry now
crossing the river

Our company started out again
with Sutter limping along behind
Roll out!
Mr. Casey shouted

Now that the Andersons had to stay in Independence
and the Lortons turned back
and Mr. Portee was gone
there were just seven of us

Sylvia
The Kansas River / August 1879

We heard the river
before we saw it
loud and roaring
like it woke up mad
and needed to tell everyone why
Rains got it high
but we'll make do
Mr. Spruill yelled to us
The men worked together
tying all the rope we had
into one long enough to reach
down the long, hilly bank
across the Kansas River

making plans for the safest
shallowest parts
to cross over
Lord you never heard so much fussing
in your life
Each one knew more than the next
How men get anything done at all
is always something got my mind turning
when they like talking more than
listening
Leading more than
following
Women know the only way to get something done
is to know when
to do which
Beau Casey said he'd head over first
with the rope
get it tied good so we all
could come across
He unyoked their team of oxen
and took them through the river

and we moved Charly and Titus
to the bank
so they could watch
A mule ain't about to do nothing
without knowing someone else did it first
They're smart that way
especially Charly
Menfolk could learn from watching him
Beau started out
with the ropes
all tied into one
wrapped round his neck
one arm holding to the team
the other pulling the rope that was tied
on our side to the wheel of a heavy wagon
We watched Beau
every step
water rising up around him and the oxen
When he went down once
and the river covered him
like a blanket
Mr. Casey yelled out
Beau! Beau!
and his head came right back up
He turned back to the bank and us
waving his arms
telling us all he was just fine
and we all clapped
like he was playacting
Each step closer to the other shore
let us know
we too would be safe crossing
with a rope to hold on to over that
Mad
Mad
river

134

Lettie
Kansas / August 1879

You scared to cross the river?
I asked Daddy
He laughed
told me

Right up until freedom
every day I woke
I was scareder than the last
Never knew what was gonna come
If I was gonna eat
gonna get a beating
be sold off
maybe all
Not knowing
is the scariest thing there is Lettie
That's why a man gotta
set his mind to making his own way
without no one telling him what he gonna do
You understand?

Yes Daddy
I told him

Last night
there was a meeting
and Momma let me sit between
her and Miss Pratt
Mr. Casey stood up high on a rock
so everyone could see him
Beau and Emmanuel sat on either side

Looks like we gonna need to wait
another day
to get across
he yelled
The river rose some
on account of the rains
Just be glad
we come when we did
not during the spring
'less we'd be waiting
a week
not a day
I could feel
everyone getting restless
the way Silas did
when he sat at the table
too long after supper

Folks down the way
taking a ferry across Amos
Miss Clara
said behind me

Now I figured
one of you be asking
'bout that ferryman
Mr. Casey said
He charging
a dollar and fifty cents a wagon
and the way I see it
not all of us here
is fit
to pay his prices
It got quiet
Daddy looked down
at his boots

But you is
Mr. Boston shouted
Why ain't you—

136

Mr. Casey put his hand up again
When we started out
we agreed
we all stick together
Don't make no difference
what I got
We started out as one
we stay as one
Daddy sat up straight
nodding his head
That's right
he said

So we give it another day
And we cross late—

I say we go first thing
Mr. Boston shouted again from the back
So we don't lose more time

His wife is sickly
and I've never once seen her outside of their wagon
Their daughters keep to themselves
and spend more time
cooking and laundering
caring for their momma
than Momma does
caring for us
But they don't seem to mind
one bit
I heard Daddy tell Momma
Make no sense bringing her along
She ain't gonna survive the first winter

Mr. Casey had to raise his voice some
so we could hear him over Mr. Boston
The sun gonna help us a little bit
warm us up
animals too
so they take more kindly
to crossing in the water
They go easier when they tired
hot
So we go later
not earlier
so first thing we gonna need to do
Take care to carry things across
You don't want to see
floating downriver
That means
letters from your sweetheart back home
Mr. Casey stopped and looked at Emmanuel
And everyone laughed a little
Pho-to-graphs of your momma
and your Bibles
Next thing
we're gonna need to lighten our wagons
Leave off the things you don't need
That's when the talk started getting loud

What we don't need Amos?

We done traveled all this way to leave our things behind?

137

I ain't leaving nothing!

One of the Cole brothers yelled next to me
Everything I got in this world in my wagon

Mr. Casey held up his hands
Waited
When the voices quieted
he pointed over to where the river was

River don't care how far you brought
your chairs
your grandpappy's chest
That there river gonna drag you down
you try to cross with a wagon too heavy

Someone shouted
Can't but a few of us swim

Mr. Casey said
Now we ain't got time
My boy got a rope tied up
real tight
from the other side of the river
Just gotta hang on tight
keep your senses
and get on across

The shouting quieted some
the questions too

Women and children first
Then each man
takes over his own wagon
Merritt?
Mr. Casey shouted to Mr. Boston
You let your girls walk across
keep Lydia in the wagon
and cross later with her
Emmanuel will stay with you
make sure your wife is safe

Mr. Boston nodded
thanking him

Everybody started standing again
heading back to their own wagons
Mr. Casey looked tired
but he looked something else too
He looked
scared

Lettie
Kansas / August 1879

I was born free
so what I knew about having a master
was what I heard
my momma and daddy
aunts and uncles
and grown folks back home talk about
over supper
whispering
crying sometimes
in the pews on Sunday mornings
I went to bed at night
with my belly full
warm in bed
next to my brothers
I woke up knowing they'd still be there
by my side every morning

Down by the river
where Uncle Benton
baptized folks
while we stood on the banks
singing
Take me to the river . . .
That same river
is where Leavitt
an older boy from school
taught me to swim
showed me how to lie on my back
in the water
my arms spread out
by my side
Make like you dead
he told me

so I did
with my head looking up
at the sky
and it felt like
a miracle
Like when Jesus
walked on water
except Leavitt said

See there, you floating

Then he showed me how to
float on my stomach
and use my arms
to move
to swim in the river
anywhere I wanted
Free
When I showed Momma and Daddy
Momma put her hand over her mouth
trying not to scream I think
and then she laughed
louder than I ever heard her
That night at supper
she told me

You show your brothers now
just what you learned in the water
You hear?
They never let us . . .
Never let us learn
afraid we start swimming
and keep right on going

With Daddy watching
I showed Elijah and Silas both
until they could swim just as good
maybe better than me
But tonight
with sleep far away
even the night sky
and remembering the feeling of floating on water
couldn't make me
stop being afraid

Sylvia
Kansas / August 1879

I held as much
of our things as I could
in a sack in my arms
Empty as our tin was
it felt heavy now
Lettie carried our Bible
Her newspaper
folded in the center
Both wrapped tight
in a blanket she tied
to her chest

Thomas told me to go on ahead
I'mma cross with the mules
our wagon
safer if you go on

You be careful
I told him
holding him to me

What else I'mma be?
He laughed
Anybody get me across
gonna be Charly and Titus
Go on take care of the children

He didn't look one bit
as scared as I was feeling
Knowing Lettie, Silas, and Elijah
could swim
gave me some comfort
even Miss Pratt told me

I do just fine in the water

I never told any one of them
it was me
scared most of all
of that rushing river

141

of water too high
of losing hold of that rope
I was just too plain scared
to cross that water

Philomena
Kansas / August 1879

I had to first get Silas and Elijah
to stop searching
through the piles
of belongings
others had left behind
before us
before their crossings
I couldn't blame them
There were toys
furniture
a mirror
in a beautiful silver frame
I would have loved for myself
But in the end
I directed them down the bank
bent down while Silas
climbed onto my back

Silas nearly choked me
his small hands were wrapped so tight
around my neck
I was glad Lettie
was tall for her age
tall enough
so that Elijah could climb onto her back
on the walk across the river
and I didn't have to take them both

You sure one of the boys
shouldn't be with you
rather than Lettie?
She's tall for her age
but you still got a few inches on her yet

I asked Miss Sylvia
early on
as we stood lined up
waiting our turn to cross
She looked shamefaced
said soft just for my ears
I'm barely going to make it 'cross myself
She choked
Don't know what I'll do
if one of them lets go
I wouldn't be able to . . .

I reached out
touched her hand

It's perfectly fine
I am quite fine in the water
and Lettie told me
she and the boys are good swimmers as well
We'll take them
and you just take your time

She held my hand
Thank you Miss Pratt

143

The water was colder
than I thought it would be
the kind of cold
that cuts through you
Sharp
I lifted the skirt of my dress
so it wouldn't drag me and Silas down

You ready?
I asked him

and we started across
I could hear his teeth
chattering in my ear

We close yet?
he kept asking

Open your eyes Silas
I said, and laughed

I can't
he told me

holding my neck tighter
The older woman in front of us
Miss Lucy I think it was
slipped
let go of the rope
made a splash in the water
and I reached forward
and righted her

Help us Jesus
she prayed and kept on

Some folks walked so slow
It seemed like it took us
hours to cross
My legs went numb
from the cold

How much more?
Silas asked again

Almost there
I lied

I turned to see how
Lettie and Elijah
Sylvia
were doing behind us
I saw Sylvia looking down
into the water
lips moving
as if she were asking the river
to quiet
and let her pass safe
She was moving so slow
a long line
waited behind her

C'mon now Sylvia
Miss Clara said behind her

What's wrong with Momma?
Silas must have heard Miss Clara

She's doing just fine
taking her time is all
Keep your eyes closed
I told him

not wanting him to see
his momma talking to a river
and all those in front of us
holding on
and walking
like every step was their last

Philomena
Kansas / August 1879

I rubbed my sore neck
after we climbed up the steep riverbank
on the other side
and wrung my dress dry
We sat in the grass
with others waiting
till everyone crossed
safe
until there was only Thomas
left to cross with the wagon
Charly and Titus
Sylvia stood watching him
holding herself tight
shivering
still in her wet clothes
as he started toward the river
folks were changing
into dry clothes
and wringing out wet ones
laughing
singing
now
when they'd been scared near witless
and silent

moments ago
I could see Thomas taking his time
tying down all the
wagon supplies with rope
making sure the fabric stretched over the top
was folded tight
together in back
keeping everything inside
for the trip across

Charly led off
looking like he'd crossed
rivers hundreds of times before
But I could see Titus
was already rearing back
not trusting
the cold
the waves
I saw Thomas grabbing the reins
saw his mouth
shouting at Titus
Hold steady now!

146

Mr. Casey asked out loud
What's that boy doing?
stepping next to me
A couple of folks stopped
their changing to watch Thomas
I could see the wagon moving away
from the rope line
away from the shallows
closer to the channel
where it was deeper

Beau!
Mr. Casey turned to his son
nodded his head at him
to the river and Thomas

He gone too far
Beau said to his father
Beau waved his hand to Thomas
shouted at him
Other way!
Closer

To
The
Rope!

If Thomas heard
it didn't seem so
He was trying hard to make
Titus listen
Trying to keep the wagon upright
Trying not to fall off
But then
doing all
one side of the wagon dropped low
into the water
Titus's eyes looked wild
his legs trying to grab ahold
of solid ground
kicking
his mouth opened wide
while the wagon kept tipping
Sylvia choked back a scream
and everyone was quiet now
Charly pulled right
with all he had
trying to steady the wagon
and now Titus
following Charly's lead
was trying too
but it was too late
for Thomas
He fell over the side of the wagon
into the water
in the channel where it was deep
and he wasn't supposed to be

Sylvia
Kansas / August 1879

My daddy can't swim!
I heard Lettie shout
Didn't even know she was behind me
but I should have known
my Lettie would be watching
She always was

Lettie
Kansas / August 1879

No one could help him
no one
but me
I pulled off my boots
Running
past Momma
over rocks and sticks
that cut my feet
as I made it

back down the steep riverbank
to the water
to my daddy

Lettie, no!
Momma shouted behind me

I jumped in
I could hear Beau Casey
swimming up on me
his heavy breathing
getting louder
and closer

Daddy! I screamed

My mouth filled with muddy water

Daddy!
I looked
where I was sure
I saw him go down
But now I wasn't so sure
because everywhere
looked the same
with only rushing water
My arms and legs
moved fast
to keep me from being
taken by the river

my head moved back
and forth
again
back
and forth
seeing nothing
but water
and the top of our wagon
But then there was
Charly's head
and Titus's
coming toward me
The wagon bouncing in the water

Go on back Lettie
Beau was saying next to me
Go on back girl

I swam closer to Charly and Titus
hoping
praying
Daddy was hanging on
to our wagon
I swam past
a boot
two cups
pots and wooden spoons
and I wasn't sure
if they were ours
or someone else's
and didn't much care
because
as hard as I swam
close enough now
to hear the huffing
from Charly and Titus
and touch the wagon
I didn't see my daddy
anywhere

149

Sylvia
Kansas / August 1879

It was Beau and Emmanuel
who pulled my Thomas
from downriver
blood still running from his head
where it had been cut open wide
by a rock, the wagon
not sure which
They laid him in the grass
his brown eyes
were open
looking at nothing
and everything
so I thought
Maybe
Just maybe . . .
But when I pressed
my head
to his wet chest
water from the Kansas River
ran from his mouth
When I whispered
into his ear
Thomas? Thomas?
he was silent
I didn't know I was shouting
until I looked up
and saw Elijah and Silas
Lettie
looking down at me
tears wetting their faces
Clara put her hands on my shoulders
tried to pull me away
from Thomas
gone to me
to all of us now
swallowed
by a river

Philomena
Kansas / August 1879

With the men
I shoveled the grave for Thomas
They told me
Sit down
This here is men's work
But there wasn't anything in my mind
that told me a woman
can't shovel dirt

honor the dead
just as good as a man
They weren't going to have me
picking flowers
and singing songs
when Sylvia could barely stand in her grief
It had been so long
since I lost my own parents
I could hardly remember
their faces
my own pain
But Elijah
Silas
Lettie
stirred in me
the heartache I know I must have felt
Picking up a shovel
digging dirt
was the very least
I could do

Lettie
Kansas / August 1879

I know—
I know, this been a long hard day
for all of us
but we got to keep on
Mr. Casey said
after they laid my daddy

in the grave
The bottom of Miss Pratt's dress
was covered in mud
after she stood right 'longside
the men shoveling
Even though Mr. Casey said
we had to move on
Momma wasn't moving
from the back of the wagon
where she's been lying
since they pulled Daddy from the river
Turns out
after all my lessons
from Leavitt back home
all my swimming
couldn't even save my daddy
and he just floated away
like the cups
plates and spoons
downriver
Mr. Casey said
We got to move on
Ain't no moving on
from my daddy being gone
from hurting
losing him
missing him
Mr. Casey said
We got to move on
But how we gonna make it
West
without my daddy?

Sylvia
Kansas / August 1879

I could hear them
outside the wagon
whispering
How?
They wanted to know
How they gonna make it
without Thomas?

Who's gonna drive their wagon?
hunt for their food?
take care of the women
children
without Thomas?
Like I wasn't nothing
without him
We come all this way
traveling West
to a new home
where I never wanted to be
I had to leave behind
everyone
everything
I ever known
for Thomas
and his dreams
I knew now
I didn't have no choice
wasn't no place for me
and my babies
but ahead
in Nebraska
with or without
my Thomas

Lettie
Kansas / August 1879

They waited
a full day
until Mr. Casey said

We ain't got no more time

while they stood together
waiting to see what we—
my momma really—
was going to do
Go forward
Go back
Stay where she was
right here in Kansas

Silas and Elijah
quit their wanderings
and stayed close to me
worried about the same things
I guess I was too
This morning
Momma woke up
as a red sun
set over the plains
like it was planning
to set the fields on fire

We're moving out today
Momma told us

Back home?
Elijah asked before I could

Momma smiled and rubbed his head
We gotta keep going baby boy
West
We all
got to be our own Moses now

154

Then I asked
You gonna drive Charly and Titus?

Momma said
I am not
She smiled
tired
sad
But Miss Pratt is

Philomena
Kansas / August 1879

What do I know
about driving a team?
About making mules mind
mile after mile?
A teacher told me
some time ago

There's nothing a smart woman
can't learn
So figuring how to drive
a team of mules
I suppose I can figure out
as easy as I did
most everything else
First thing
I found Lettie
and had her make my acquaintance
once again
with Charly and Titus

Right here?
I pointed at Charly's nose
she smiled then
as I bent over
and brushed my lips
quick as I could against his nose
That's not a kiss
she told me

I don't want to marry him
I just need him to mind me

He will
Won't you Charly?
Lettie said
Her face pressed into his neck
It was good to see
something could make her happy
after losing her daddy
I climbed up
into the wagon seat
took the reins in my hands
Even though I'd only driven
to and from town
with our wagon
and horses
I had to do the best I could
with my fast learning
Lettie
Charly and Titus
Sylvia's trust

and God
if I was going to
get us all
West

Lettie
Kansas / August 1879

Momma says we're ready to go
and Miss Pratt
is already sitting in the seat
where Daddy used to
She says I can ride next to her
for part of the way
but no one asked
if I was ready
to leave behind my daddy
buried next to the river
that took him from me
I can't remember now
what he said last
The last time he made me laugh
called me his *baby girl*
I can still smell him though
in his clothes
Momma keeps in a sack
The smell of woodsmoke
and the tobacco he chewed sometimes
How can I be ready to go
if I still keep waiting
for him
and hearing his voice
all around?
Who is going to sit by his resting place
when we move on?
Tell him if Elijah and Silas
are acting right?
How Momma is making do?
Ask him about the night sounds?
Tell him what Nebraska looks like?
If it is everything he dreamed?
Who will tell him
if we leave him behind?

The other wagons
that pass
on their way West
will see his name
Thomas Grier
Born 1845
Died 1879
carved deep
into two sticks
crossed in the middle
and never even know
he was more than dirt
and sticks
He was my daddy

Sylvia
Kansas / August 1879

All I knew
was what I was being called
to do
by God
by faith
I had to make my way
to the Promised Land
of the West
of Thomas
There wasn't going to be
no turning around
alone
with just me
and my babies
trying to make it back
to Mississippi
As long as I had the strength
to keep moving
that's just what I would do
Lettie
the boys
were hurting same as me
but staying still
wasn't no choice
Miss Pratt

shown herself to be
the woman I wish I was
No one makes her mind up
but her
Hoping my Lettie see more of that kind
and less of mine
When the mens
were worrying over my future
was Miss Pratt
that told them
and me
wasn't no need for worrying
when she could very well
drive our mules and wagon
Mr. Casey near fell out
but he
and the others learned today
a woman
who got no one but herself
who got educated enough to be a teacher
saved her own money
can swim
shovel dirt for a grave
is a woman
who don't need
men
to make her way West

158

PART FOUR

. . . .

On Jordan's stormy banks I stand
And cast a wishful eye
To Canaan's fair and happy land
Where my possessions lie
I am bound for the Promised Land
I am bound for the Promised Land
Oh, who will come and go with me?
I am bound for the Promised Land . . .

—"On Jordan's Stormy Banks I Stand,"

hymn by Samuel Stennett, 1787

Lettie
Entering Nebraska
August 1879

I tried to write all I saw
in my book
the grasshoppers hopping with every step
I took
the robins finding their way back home
in the sky
the tall prairie grasses
the deer and elk
Once even a herd of buffalo
and mountains that looked
like a dull knife cut them out of the sky
But mostly I wrote now
because I couldn't find the words
to say all I was feeling
Momma kept fussing over me
making sure I was eating
talking more than she had
in all the months

we been traveling
trying to fill in
the space Daddy left behind
Nighttime used to be my favorite part of the day
staring into the stars
in the dark sky
but last night
when I was too tired
to look at the stars and moon
is when Daddy came
his big voice
laughing in my ear

I thought you were gone?
I said to him

Gone where?
He laughed again
Ain't going nowhere without my baby girl
I felt his arms around me
his breath on my face

I could hardly believe
God brought him back to me
to us
I wanted to run
tell Momma, Silas, and Elijah
but when I opened my eyes
I saw two small ones staring back
Felt a cold, wet nose
against mine
that wasn't my daddy's
Sutter?
He whined
stood shaking
so I pulled him close
tucked him in under my blanket
till his shivering stopped
That's when
I let the tears go
into his patchy fur
stiff with dirt
We're gonna be all right Sutter
I told him
hoping with everything
it was true
I remembered then
Sutter had to leave his daddy behind
buried in the ground
just like me

Philomena
Nebraska / August 1879

Do you believe in ghosts?
Lettie asked me this morning
as we started out
It was the first I'd heard her speak
in days
Her voice was scratchy
like it had forgotten
what it was supposed to do
Ghosts?
Well I know
there are a good number of folks

who put a lot of stock in the things they can't see
coming back from beyond
Haints
I think my aunt Perlie called them
But me
I figure it's hard enough for our people
when we're on this side of the dirt
why would we ever come back?
Lettie got quiet again
making me wonder
if I said too much

Ain't everyone as interested in your opinion
as you are
Aunt Perlie told me nearly every day
Her way of telling me
I knew too much for my own good
Out ahead
Were miles of prairie
and even though Mr. Casey
had us starting earlier than I ever rose at home
to get in the miles we needed
and lost

162

before the animals
needed their watering and feeding
I didn't mind a bit
It was the part of the day
when the fog hung low
over the prairie
like the pretty lace curtains
hung at the windows
of rich folks' homes in town
And you could just make out
the miles ahead
of flat land
that looked as if it had no imagination
for itself
because it only chose
one color to be
when there were so many
blues, greens
reds and pinks
it forgot about
Looking out

across the acres
I let my mind
think well past
the weeks
and months ahead
and into my life
in Nebraska
with not one soul
telling me what to do with my day
and to keep my opinions
to myself

Sylvia
Nebraska / August 1879

Wasn't much that could stop my Lettie
from asking
laughing
spending her day
chattering about one thing
or the other
but I feel now
in losing Thomas
I am losing Lettie too

Silas and Elijah
been making their way
as they do
two boys
one mind
Because they always have each other
they manage to get through most things
Seems sitting up with Miss Pratt
in the wagon seat
might be doing Lettie some good
especially since she put Mr. Portee's
dirty little dog
alongside her
holding him tight
like he was one of her rag dolls
afraid to let him go
Thomas would have fussed at her
to let that dog loose

nasty as he is
more mud and dirt than fur
But seeing her
warming to something
tells me
just maybe
not all of her
was buried with Thomas
miles back
There's still some of my Lettie's heart
beating strong

Lettie
Nebraska / August 1879

I got used to the smell of
stink and mud and mules
but Momma never did
making us wash
every few days
instead of every few weeks
like most did
Momma had me head down by the creek
where we stopped to water the animals
While they were drinking their fill
and Mrs. Day, Miss Clara, and Miss Dottie
were doing their washing
I got in
with Sutter under my arm
he kicked
barked
tried to jump out of my arms
but I held tight
singing soft in his pointy ears
till he calmed
Standing in the creek
I rubbed the little piece of lye soap
Momma gave me
over my neck, arms and legs
then all over his fur
But standing in the water
made me think again of Daddy
his head going under

So fast as I could
I scooped my hand
to rinse off
and then
with as much water as Sutter would let me
rinsed out the soap from his fur
then we got out
and sat in the grass
I wrapped him in cloth Momma gave me
dried him good as I could
and his fur stuck up every which way
but I rubbed it smooth
and when it was dry and flat
and shiny
he looked like a whole different dog
Sutter laid his head in my lap
yawned
and watched
the creek with me
calm
Funny how
things can be so ugly
one minute
like Sutter
and the water
And can look so pretty
the next

Sylvia
Nebraska / August 1879

With Miss Pratt as the driver
Lettie up front with her
working right 'longside to help
with Charly and Titus
I had no choice
but to walk
keeping hold of Silas
and Elijah
lest I let the wind
take them
Each
held to my skirts

as we walked
our heads down low
if you didn't know better
you'd think we were praying
though I was doing that plenty
Wasn't no way
we were going to make the miles
Amos said we needed to do today
Twenty
Yesterday neither
Every day we were falling
further behind
for one reason or another
the wind
the rain
took too much time at the last fort
restocking our supplies
Last week
the tongue of Marshall's wagon
broke in two
and the men spent a full day
fixing it

Lydia Boston and her youngest daughter Heloise took a turn
the week before
with fevers running high
her daughter Ellen
came running to Dottie
in the middle of the night for nursing
We been hearing about cholera
spreading through companies
killing near every single one
and we were all afraid
to move ahead
to go near the Bostons
and help like Dottie did
Just maybe it was starting to spread
through ours?
But when the day was out
come morning
both women were feeling fine
and Amos called us out
The one thing we didn't have
Time
was wasting away

Today was just the tiredness
and fighting back
the wind
and praying
every step of the way

Lettie
Nebraska / September 1879

Charly and Titus
took to Miss Pratt
just fine
They were missing Daddy
I know
but I know too
they figured
their job was to get us
where we needed to be
and wasn't nothing
or no one
gonna stop them from doing that

Sometimes
Miss Pratt needed reminding
about the things
they did and didn't like
And even though
she was pretty soon going to be a teacher and all
there was a lot she needed teaching in
about Charly and Titus

I taught her to watch their ears
and the way they picked up their heads
just so
because long before we could
their ears heard
and their noses smelled
what we couldn't
coyote
bears
and what-all else
was out there waiting
or coming our way

And sometimes
Miss Pratt did a little too much
talking for her own good
so I taught her that Charly and Titus
liked when you said things real plain
When she shouted to them
over the reins
Go on now
to get them going faster up a hill
it was like she was telling them
two different things
at once
because Charly and Titus heard
Whoa on now
and they'd stop right there in their tracks
just like they were supposed to
You just need to say
Go
Miss Pratt
short and sweet
or
Whoa
That's how they like it
Daddy told me once
You don't so much talk to a mule
as sing to them
And even though she was a woman
I told her she needed to make her
words deep and low
like a man's
like my daddy's

Philomena
Nebraska / September 1879

How you making out with the driving
Miss Pratt?
Beau Casey asked after my first week

How does it look like I'm doing?
I asked him back
I'll take to it
No other choice I suppose
I told him

You need any help
You just let me know
He tipped his hat
Lettie walked over
with my supper plate
and I found a place
to sit by the fire
It hurt to even bend
let alone sit
worse than the walking almost
after riding all day on the hard bench
of the wagon
leaned forward
holding reins
shouting to Charly and Titus
But for the sake of everyone
I knew I had to keep pretending
I was as good at wagoneering
as any of the men
Pretending I wasn't hurting in places
I didn't know could hurt
pretending I didn't want to cry
pretending I didn't think every morning
about turning back
and Lord help me
pretending I didn't notice Beau Casey's
bright smile
full lips
skin so smooth and brown
about as pretty as oiled leather

Lettie
Nebraska / September 1879

Are you and Beau Casey courting?
I asked Miss Pratt

She picked up the reins
I'm not interested in courting Lettie
She smiled down at me and Sutter

I see the two of you talking
and whenever he's talking
you smile a lot

Well that's just called being polite
Miss Pratt told me
in a way teachers do

I understand about polite
I told her
Momma said you have good manners
so you must have come from a good family
in Independence
Is that true?
If Momma wasn't up ahead with Miss Clara
I surely wouldn't have been so bold
with my questions

I'd say so yes

You are very polite with
Mr. Casey
I said
Miss Pratt nodded
And Mr. Day
Mr. Lorton and Mr. Boston
when you talk to them

She laughed
Your mother is right Lettie
You are very observant
Did you write all this down in your book
Who I am polite to?

But the only person you smile at
is Beau Casey
I told her
That's the part
I wrote down
in my book

Lettie
Nebraska / September 1879

When I wasn't writing
or telling Miss Pratt
how to talk to Charly and Titus
She asked me to read to her

from the book she brought in her satchel
to pass the time
as we bumped along
through the prairie grasses
of Kansas
I lifted the skirt of my dress
to let the wind blow on
my scratched-up legs
torn to bits by the grasses
that looked like they'd be soft
tickling us like
feathers
when we first stepped through
but instead
they stuck to the hem
of my dress
pulling
like fingernails
scratching

My legs are itching
Silas complained all day

You got to pay it no mind
Momma told him

But I could see her scratching too
just like we were
At night
Momma spread the salve
she brought for our trip
on our arms and legs
so we smelled like mint
and camphor all day
I left Sutter
up in the wagon seat
next to Miss Pratt
if I was walking
I didn't much care she didn't take kindly
to animals
Sutter was likely to get lost
in the tall grasses
or cut up
in the places his fur was gone

Just for a little while?
I asked Miss Pratt

Hmmmphh she said
to the reins

But the times I sat up next to her
with Sutter on my lap
reading
she said

Your momma was right
you are a good reader

I tried not to be prideful
but I was
Hearing Miss Pratt
a real teacher
instead of just my momma and daddy
or Miss Rowser
our teacher at school
who told everybody
the same thing
because there were so many of us
squeezed together on benches
and chairs
in our small schoolhouse
she hardly had the time to help one
before someone else needed help too
Miss Pratt saying I was a good reader
got me to thinking
about not just pretending
being a teacher
like I did with Oda
but being one
like her

Some days
I read
the book she brought
A story I didn't much like
but tried to pretend I did
On other days

I read my newspaper
wrinkled as it was
some pages so worn
I had to squint my eyes
to read the words now
There were words
I didn't know
and Miss Pratt would say
Take your time Lettie
That's a difficult one

Or I could spell out a word
And she would tell me
just how to say it
or even what it meant

Do you know every word?
I asked her

I certainly do not Lettie
But the more you read
the more words you'll know

I liked the way she talked
like no one I ever heard before
not even Miss Rowser
my teacher back home
who was smart
but I could tell
not nearly as smart
as Miss Pratt

I held the newspaper tight against the wind
folded it in a square
to keep it from blowing away
because when I read
I remembered
it was the last time
I was alone with my daddy
and it was all
I had left
to show for it

Philomena

Nebraska / September 1879

Beau had nineteen years
to my eighteen
He had a fair share of schooling
but not nearly as much as I did
He told me his daddy
Mr. Casey saw to it that he and his brother Emmanuel
kept up with their schooling
Their momma had some education
taught by her master's wife
and she taught their daddy, Mr. Casey
what she knew
and then her boys
But after she passed

I miss her every day
Beau told me

Their daddy sent them to school
when he didn't need help in the fields
And when he did
he sat with them at the table at night
tired
with the worn-out books
their momma had at the house
going over their letters and numbers
like their momma would have wanted

One day
this is gonna be all yours
Only way you keep it
is knowing enough
to know how to keep it
That's what our daddy told us
just about every day
Beau said

You're lucky you had land
to own
to sell
Not many of us do
I told him

It wasn't easy
Beau said back quick
My daddy had to fight for every acre
He's thinking out West
a man with a good mind for business
can go far
Help us to get set up too
not like back home

I liked the sound of his voice
Soft but
deep

Ain't you young to be a teacher?
he asked me then
smiling
that pretty smile of his
I thought then of my schoolhouse
And my teacher
Miss Farber
Who made me stay in school
When Aunt Perlie told me I had enough
for a girl
Even Uncle Edmund
who tried his best
to stand up for me
asked me

What more do you need to learn Philomena?
you already know your letters and numbers
don't you?
That's more than most

But it was Miss Farber
who sometimes let me nap
in the corner
while the other students were working
on slates
just because she knew I had worked
nearly all night
mopping floors

Just try to catch up on your lessons
when you can
she told me

We can't have that bright mind of yours
going to waste

By the time I finished my schooling
I was the oldest girl student she had
All the others had left
for work
or marriage and children

She sent off a letter
to an aunt
who had moved to Nebraska
asking if she knew anyone in need
of a bright young teacher
and a school sent a letter right back
asking after me
I'll never forget
standing in that schoolroom
one year ago
when Miss Farber handed me that letter
her smile
as big as mine

Young or not
I'm qualified
I told him

Didn't mean nothing by it—

He could see the hurt
the anger
the fight
in my eyes

Just that
I never had a teacher—

I could feel the eyes
of everyone in the company
on us
pretending to be eating
and doing nothing
but watching
and trying their best

to listen in
to hear Beau's quiet voice

I never had a teacher
as pretty as you

I didn't know if it was the heat
or his words
but I thought I would
melt right there

Lettie
Nebraska / September 1879

I wait for Daddy
every night as I lie
staring at the sky
I look for him
in the stars
listen
for the sound of his voice
in the barking of coyote
and the steady beeping
of creeping bugs
and squawking birds
The sandpiper
Mr. Cole told me
who makes it his business
to tell me
all I don't know
about the land
we left
and the land
we're going to
in Nebraska

This here learning
you not likely to find
in that newspaper I see you reading
he told me
Outside learning
what keeps folks alive
not words

Momma told me his girl
moved North
some time ago
After he lost his wife
he and his brother Oscar
been running their farms alone
ever since

It's been some time
since Hark's seen his girl
I suspect you favor her in some way Lettie
just let him talk
So I do

Over and over again
Those sandpipers sing out
keeping time
like we do in the pews
on Sunday morning
singing hymns
like the ones
Momma hums to herself
when she works
cooks
worries
I wait
but most nights
Daddy never comes
It is just me
and the sky
the birds and bugs
and Sutter
curled in close
and breathing heavy in my arms
warming me

My good boy
I whisper in his little crooked ear
watching it twitch
under my breath

Is he your dog now?
Silas asked me yesterday

He sure is
He's all mine
I told him

Well your dog smells bad
Elijah told me
the two of them ran off laughing

Sutter never leaves my side now
He goes with me hunting for firewood
and when Momma sends me
to fetch water
he's right there with me
As much as his hind leg is hurting
he never slows his walking
as long as he's beside me
one time even barking
when a black snake
came crawling from out of a bush
where I was picking berries
scaring him back into the bush

You keeping me safe Sutter?
I asked him
hugging him tight around his neck
It was likely
he was missing Mr. Portee
sure as I was missing my daddy
but I think he found
because you loved one
didn't mean you couldn't love
another

Sutter was running again
in his sleep
What was he dreaming?
I wondered
That he was young
on four good legs
digging
chasing rabbits
and squirrels?
That Mr. Portee was alive?

179

I wondered if he dreamed
the way I dreamed
of my daddy
so clear
I could feel the roughness of his hands
scratching
my arms when held me

There was no sign of Daddy tonight
but holding tight to Sutter
under my blanket
I wondered
Could Daddy be . . .
not in the
sky
and stars
like I thought
but here
right alongside me
looking after me
every day
keeping me company
keeping me safe
in Sutter?

Sylvia
Nebraska / September 1879

Momma I'm cold
Silas told me this morning
coming into my tent
his blanket wrapped tight around him
before my eyes were barely open
I got up
to get a fire started
An early frost covered our camp
and our bucket of water
just enough
so that
there was ice
in our water pail
I had to crack
to get at the water
underneath

Miss Pratt had the good sense
to cover Charly and Titus
with their blankets last night
before we turned in
or they might have been frozen too
I came back to my tent
and pulled Silas in my bedroll with me
and wished I hadn't
He tucked his thumb
in his mouth
fell back to sleep
The little warmth he had
put me in the mind of
remembering
just when I'd gotten good
at forgetting
of all I'd lost
left behind
My family
my Thomas
the warmth
the smell and sound
the safety
of him
Knowing I didn't have no one
now
but me to count on
Sometimes I lay awake
half the night
William said
Kearney ain't but
a little more
than two weeks away
if we make good time
three if we don't
So close
to all Thomas dreamed of
and now
so far away for him
but not for us
I can feel
I can imagine now
some of what Thomas must have
all those months ago
sitting at our table

Ain't got to know nothing
he said to me
as I was fixing his breakfast plate
like he was talking to the children
to our mules, cows, and chickens
like he was the master
and I was the slave
All you got to know is they giving out land
to anyone who wants it
white or colored
We'd be homesteaders
I fixed my own plate
sat down at his side
We going to go all the way West
all by ourselves?
What about our family?
My family?

Mouth full of food
he answered me

Wouldn't be going alone
We'd join up with a wagon company
Hear the Days is going
Caseys too
Folks we know
who can see like I can
some other families be leaving out of
Vicksburg
Your sister
her family, your brothers
free to join us
hitch on to our company they see fit
He took a bite from his plate

Thomas, I don't see how we going to leave behind—
wiped his mouth

You living for your brothers and sister
or you living for me?
I put my head down

I'm doing this for us
Elijah, and Silas

for our Lettie
Wagon train leaving in two weeks
We need to be ready to go then

Two weeks
I remember
how my food stuck in my throat

If I learned one thing
it was
in order to keep going
you had to forget
Think only of
tomorrow
and never of
yesterdays
and todays
cold
hunger
loneliness
anger
and
loss
The tomorrows
was how we always
made it through
every hard time
trusting
that God
will see us through
another day
We'll get our just reward
If not here in this life
then for sure
tomorrow
in the Promised Land

Lettie
Nebraska / September 1879

You listening Sutter?
Sutter's crooked ear
was leaning forward

183

his head tilted to the side
as we sat
outside of our camp
my back leaned against
a big rock
Sutter leaned against me
The grasses
were worn down here
by wagons
oxen
feet passing through
so we could sit and almost feel
the hard dirt
underneath
I liked to find a quiet place
to write down
my words
and now
I could read them
out loud
to Sutter
if he was in the mood
Today he was just in the mood
for listening
and catching the scent
of the squirrels
that ran past
every now and again
and I'd have to grab him
around his neck
so he wouldn't go chasing

Settle down now
I told Sutter
rubbing down the fur
that was rising up
on his back
He was wanting to go hunting
I could tell
just like Silas
but since Mr. Portee passed
the men wouldn't take him
You gonna wanna hear this—

184

Your dog bite?

I heard behind me
I turned
It was Agnes Day
the older girl from my school
whose brother Earl
was born the same time
same day
Twins
Momma told me
even though they didn't look nothing
alike
like Momma said twins do
Whether boy and girl
or not
Agnes and Earl
must have kept each other good company
'cause every time you saw them
it looked like
they were tied together
with rope
and couldn't get loose
Not like me
with my brothers
trying to stay as far away
from each other as we could
Even Miss Rowser
let them sit
side by side in the schoolroom too
when everybody knew
it was supposed to be
girls on one side
boys on the other

All along the trail
Momma told me

*Why don't you go on
catch up to Agnes
and walk with her
Bet she'd make a fine friend
You don't need to be
up under me all day*

But every time I tried
thinking
there wasn't no one else
out here on the trail
just us two girls
Maybe now
she'd pay me the attention
that she wouldn't
back home
and in the schoolhouse
But still
here on the trail
she turned away from me
and to her brother
like I wasn't even there
until now

I looked behind Agnes
for Earl
but didn't see him
Where's Earl?
I asked her

He's with my daddy
hunting
Daddy said
it's time he learned

Sutter doesn't bite
I told her
unless you're a snake

Well
I'm hardly a snake
She stepped closer
He looks mean
she said

Not one person
could find a kind word
to say about Sutter
I was thinking
when Agnes said

But his eyes
are sweet
and I love
his little crooked ears

Me too
I told her
scratching them
the way he liked
but Sutter pulled away
and limped over to her
laid his head
against her leg

Sutter here
I told her
is a good judge of character
He's never wrong

Lettie
Nebraska / September 1879

The way the moon hung
in the sky
it was shining
bright as a lantern
so bright
I couldn't see the stars
I stayed awake with it
writing longer
in my book
It was easier now
on account of Silas and Elijah
sleeping in the tent with Momma
They said
they didn't want to have to share a tent
with a dog
'Specially one who snores
half the night
growls the other
Sutter hears things outside
I told Momma

He can't help his nature
Momma looked down at Sutter
mad
sad
or proud
I couldn't tell

I'll keep your brothers with me
for now
she said
But you gonna have to find
some other place
for Sutter to sleep at night

I didn't tell Momma
that sometimes
his paw licking
scratching
and biting the parts
where he itched
near drove me out the tent at night too
When Momma was busy
washing clothes
down at the creek with Miss Dottie
I took the salve from our chest
and rubbed it in on the parts
Sutter scratched and bit

Tonight I had a lot of writing to do
Instead of the stars
I needed the moonlight
bright
and Sutter quiet

Mrs. Boston passed today
I read out loud to Sutter
He was tired
but stayed awake
Just like
Daddy said she would
We only knew she passed
because we all heard her daughters
Miss Arlene, Miss Ellen, and Miss Heloise
crying together

outside their wagon
Momma went right over
came back and told us
Peaceful
she said
No pain
I stopped writing
and told Sutter
That's what grown folks say
to let you know
if God calls you home
in your sleep
that's the best way
because then
you never really know
you died
you just wake up
in God's arms

Sutter looked like
he knew just what I meant
And we were both
maybe a little sad
because that's not
how Mr. Portee
and my daddy died
They died
Not peaceful
I kept writing

They're gonna bury her in the morning
I never once talked to her
I don't think most anyone did
she was that sick
Even Mrs. Abrams
Miss Clara's mother
who is the oldest person
I ever seen
walks most days
with her walking stick
slow and stiff
but keeps going still
Poor Mrs. Boston
made it this far

with her family
caring and cooking for her
only to be buried
in a field of grass
alone
Mrs. Boston
will wake up in God's arms
but just like Daddy
and Mr. Portee
She's never going to see Nebraska
But there's still seven families

I closed my book
Sutter closed his eyes

Philomena
Nebraska / October 1879

There was a rabbit
in the dinner pot tonight
thanks to Beau
Thought y'all could use it
he said to me

What I could use
is someone to teach me to trap one
myself
He stood back
hands on his hips
Staring

Is that a yes
I asked

He nodded
And you're welcome
he said
walking back
quick as he came
But still looking at me
not smiling his Beau smile
I knew I'd forgotten my manners

Was it the travel?
Being away
on my own?
Or just who I was
and was always going to be?
What everybody
back home said I was
Unwomanly
Rude
But maybe it was
Beau?
And feeling things I hadn't
ever before?
Thank you!
I shouted to his back
Too late

Lettie
Nebraska / October 1879

When Mrs. Boston's grave was dug
and everyone's wagon
was packed
and Mr. Casey
gave the call to move out
Agnes waited for me
at a bend in the road
Earl was up ahead
with their momma and daddy
Agnes said
but figured
she'd walk with me and Sutter
for a spell
Momma pushed me forward
toward Agnes
Easy
so no one could tell
Only I knew
what Momma was wanting
me to have a friend
besides Charly
and Sutter

I see you writing sometimes
Agnes said

I keep an accounting
for my momma and dad—
for my momma
I said

I'm sorry about your daddy
So all you're writing
in your book
is numbers?

I didn't know Agnes
not enough
to tell her
all I write

Mostly
I said

I miss school
she said
But Earl don't
said the last thing he wants
is to be sitting up
on some hard bench
hearing Miss Rowser talk
about history
and some such
We laughed together

I hardly remembered
the sound of my own laughing

As me and Agnes walked
we talked
about folks back home
Her cousin Surrey
and Vivvy and Oda
And folks here
Mr. Anderson
Mr. Portee
the Lortons

a little bit about my daddy
Independence, Missouri
the heat of the day
the stars at night
the fingers of the prairie grass
pulling at our skirts
Hot skillet bread
on a cold morning
the tiredness
our feet
And it was the first time
I could remember
on the trail
I lost count
of the miles

Philomena
Nebraska / October 1879

You ain't asking
I know
But if you was
I'd tell you
A man don't want to feel like
he's knocking on the door
to an empty house

Pardon Miss Sylvia?
I asked
Polite as I could
but not taking in
her meaning

She breathed long
and deep
at me
much like my aunt Perlie
used to
then laughed out loud
Now Philomena
Beau done did everything
but ask you to marry
and did I hear you ask him

about teaching you to trap rabbits
and hunting?
Only thing he wants to trap
is you

I felt the heat in my face
Well . . .

You never courted before?
Miss Sylvia asked me

I never had the time
with my schooling and all—

Well you got nothing but time
now
Miss Sylvia told me
Be home
next time he come calling

How exactly . . .
How exactly do I do that?

She laughed louder this time
than she did the last
Open your heart
and you'll open
the door
Miss Sylvia was right
I hadn't asked
but she told me
everything I wanted to know

Sylvia
Nebraska / October 1879

First time I met Thomas
he was out searching for a place to land
He come through town
asking if anyone needed a field hand
Swore he could do just about anything
Come to find out
that wasn't all truth

just talk
to get him food in his belly
a place to lay his head for the night
But finally
Mr. Casey
who was raising his two young boys

on his own
after losing his wife years back
who owned over twenty acres
finally took him on
Said
I could use some help
bringing in the crop
Things work out
I'll see about keeping you on

He fixed a pallet for Thomas
with the animals
out in his barn
away from the house
He didn't know Thomas
and you don't mix strangers
with family
I'd see Thomas in the fields next to ours
standing
hands on his hips
wiping his brow
head back
looking dead on at the sun

What's he always looking at?
My sister Olivia asked

Didn't none of us know
Mr. Casey made attending Sunday service
part of his payment

Don't house no heathens
he told Thomas

so I'd see him on Sundays
and one day after church ended
he come over to me

195

hat in his hand
smile on his lips

Seen you
he said
watching me

His words made me feel things
I never had before

Wasn't watching you
I told him
I was minding my own business
You need to be minding yours
smiling back
bold

Maybe you is my business
he told me

The day's heat spread
through me
like fire
He had nothing
didn't even know his letters
but he made it seem like that was just
a matter of circumstance
When we talked on Sundays
and on our walks after service
I could feel all he could be
would be
and that was enough for me

Lettie
Nebraska / October 1879

A family of red-tailed hawks
passed above us today
Heading back the other way
we were coming from
I wanted to shout
Come
Come with us West

But it was too late
They were already
well on their way
and couldn't no one stop them
just like us
Because of Mr. Cole
I looked up during
the day
instead of only
at night
Because of Mr. Cole
I knew now
the sounds
of the woodpeckers
horned larks
I always knew
the hoot of an owl
But Mr. Cole
knew one from the other
barn from horned
One high like a scream
the other
low like a horn
deep and far away
I watched now
the way
no matter how hard it rained
A spider's house
their web
stayed pretty
on the cottonwood trees
the raindrops
sparkling
like stars
from each tiny string

Together
after supper
when Agnes went to eat with her family
Sometimes me and Mr. Cole
and Sutter
watched the bats
at dusk
so many

they sometimes turned the pink sky
black
Like they eating up the sky
Mr. Cole said
Tonight
when we were sitting out
our backs resting
against a wagon wheel
Mr. Cole reached over
to rub Sutter's head
half asleep now
What did he care about
bats eating up
a pink sky?

Tom told me
he had ole Sutter here
since he was a pup
runt of the litter
he said
Didn't no one want him
they turned him loose
and left him to die
Mr. Cole said
This dog saved Tom's life
more than once as I recall
Maybe he was thankful
that Tom saved his
All the scrapes
they got into
shame he couldn't save him
from that last one

He's my good boy
I said quiet
thinking about poor Mr. Portee
and his last scrape

You doing a good thing
looking after him
He laughed now
They say a cat got nine lives
but this dog

keeps right on living
maybe ole Sutter
got nine lives too

Lettie
Nebraska / October 1879

My daddy say
won't be long
before we'll be in Kearney
and sooner still
in Grand Island
Agnes told me
We didn't look at each other
we both walked quiet
knowing that would mean
we'd be saying goodbye
after all these long miles together

The weather
was turning cooler
every day
just enough
that Momma had me wear
woolen stockings
and a sweater
each morning
But there were days
every now and then
when it warmed
just enough
so I could take them off
I saw Agnes had on new boots
her daddy bought
at the last fort
where we stopped for more supplies
She had worn clean through
her last pair
Earl too
And even though
my boots had holes
and were thin as paper

at the toe
I couldn't think about asking
Momma for new ones
with what little
we had left in our tin
I hoped she was too busy
to notice all I needed
and see how Elijah's pants
couldn't be mended over
any more than they were
at least
after we were through
Silas could wear
what we couldn't
When we stopped for supper
I rubbed Charly and Titus
down extra
to get them good and warm
before we started out
Titus so he'd be less cranky
Charly so he'd remember
I loved him still
Even if I spent more time now
with Sutter than him

They were both taking
to Miss Pratt though
though not Sutter
who made them huff
every time he came near
and Miss Pratt wouldn't say it
but I think
she was taking to them too
talking sweet
when she didn't have to
and she thought
no one was listening
sweeter than Daddy ever did
at least

Instead of feeling
like I thought I should

about finally
after all these months
making our way
West
and being close
to the place
we'd finally call
our new home
the place my daddy
had dreamed of
I was feeling
something else

That night
I waited
until I knew Elijah and Silas
would be sleeping good
Sutter woke when I got up
to leave
I told him
I'll be back
Stay here boy
He put his head back down
on his paws
and closed his eyes
probably thinking
I had to go make water
I went to Momma's tent
and heard talking
Momma was up too
Is Miss Pratt in her tent?
But the closer I got
I could only hear Momma's voice
and the only one
Momma was talking to
was God
I waited until I heard her say

Amen
And then I said quiet

Momma
It's me Lettie

201

Lettie?
she said
coming to the tent flap
You all right?

Yes
But I gotta talk to you
The tent was so small
but Momma pulled me in
to the side
best as she could
away from Elijah and Silas
curled into each other
just like at home
Momma said
Something happen to Sutter?

No he's sleeping

What then?

Momma . . .
Agnes said . . .
Her daddy said
that it's not gonna be long
before . . .
before we get
to where we're going
and have to say goodbye
to everyone

If we keep time yes
that's what they saying
Momma said
smoothing down my hair

But first
The Bostons
are leaving us
to be with their family
Nice little town I hear
not far from ours

Momma . . .
What are we gonna do?
How are we gonna farm?
How are we gonna live
with just us?
Without Daddy?

I could hardly see Momma
in the dark
looking at me
but she was
for a long time it felt like

You old enough to know Lettie
You asking questions
I ain't got answers to
All I can do now
All we can both do
is put our trust in God
she whispered
You trust God
don't you Lettie?

Yes ma'am

Pray with me then

I bowed my head
Momma reached for my hand
in the dark

Philomena
Nebraska / October 1879

Beau stood behind me
his mouth
in one straight line as I tied the cord
into a noose
for my trap
pulled it through the wood
and set my rock in place
Beau reached over

More like this here
he said
making the knot tighter
than I had it
My chest felt tight
when he got close
like I imagine
the rabbit was gonna feel
caught in the trap

You bound to catch one
in no time
Beau said

I thought about what Miss Sylvia told me
about opening the door

I said turning to him
I'll bet
we likely won't be able
to eat all the rabbits
I'm going to catch
with this trap

Is that so?
Beau said

I turned to him
Thank you Beau
I said
smiling big
open
You're a very good teacher

Good as you?
he asked

Well
let's see how many rabbits I catch
and I'll let you know
I laughed
and Beau finally
smiled back

Lettie

Nebraska / October 1879

Elijah's cough
started just short of midday
It had warmed up some
and I was liking
having the warmth
of the sun on my face again
after days of cold
and gray
and clouds
and woolen stockings
Miss Pratt was way up ahead
She was getting
near as good as Daddy
at driving our wagon
Last night
I read to Sutter
that I wondered
if she rode that fast
because she liked driving
and having the feeling of the wind
against her
or
because she was trying
to stay close
behind the wagon Beau was driving
for his daddy
They hunted together
and she kept us fed now
with plenty of rabbits
sometimes
even birds
and grouse
with the traps she set
One time she caught a snake for supper
that Silas and Elijah
wouldn't even touch
Miss Pratt and Beau
ate together
near every day now
and just like

Agnes and Earl
Silas and Elijah
they looked like
they had a rope
tying the two of them
together

Well good for you
Philomena
I heard Momma whispering to her

almost like she did
with Miss Clara
like they had a secret
like Miss Pratt
had just won
a spelling bee
when all she really won
was Beau Casey
which as far as I could tell
wasn't any great prize
Sutter was snoring
when I got to that part

Elijah ain't feeling so good
Silas grabbed ahold of my arm

When we were walking
and I looked back to see
Elijah had stopped
bent over
coughing
I went to him
rubbed his back
with Silas looking on
his eyes
staring wide
filling with water
Momma was up ahead
with Miss Clara
Miss Clara's mother in the middle
they were walking beside her
slow
but talking over her head

Go get Momma
I told him

and he took off
running

Agnes said
I'll fetch him some water

And she took off running too
Elijah's coughing
sounded like the blue herons
we see from time to time
barking their calls
to each other
across the plains

Elijah
Elijah
I said

When he took a break
from his coughing
I stood him up
and wiped his mouth clean
His cheeks were hot
but not from the day's sun
I put my arm around him
and had him walk with me
I was going to have to ask Agnes
to send word ahead
to Miss Pratt
to slow down
we'd need to get Elijah
in back of the wagon
so he could rest
I could see Agnes
running back
dipper in her hand
and water running
over the sides
Earl was right behind her

207

Drink this
she said
holding it to Elijah's mouth
but he turned his head away

You got to drink
I told him
to stop that coughing

Maybe you just try a little . . .
Agnes said
holding it to his mouth again

Maybe he don't want none
Earl said

And me and Agnes looked at him
our eyes saying
he wasn't helping none
But then Momma and Silas were right there
beside us
Lord Jesus
Momma was saying
Lord Jesus

Just this morning
They were playing wheelbarrow
with Elijah
holding on to Silas's
legs
and Silas walking on his hands
till a stone got stuck in his palm
and he fell
flat on his face
Only Elijah
could make Silas laugh
when he wanted to cry
but Elijah
spit on Silas's hands
wiped them clean
told Silas

Get up
I'll be the wheelbarrow
this time

But Silas couldn't lift Elijah's heavy legs
and they laughed some more at that

Y'all gotta keep up now
Stop with that playing
Momma said

That wasn't but two hours ago

By the time
we got Elijah in the back of our wagon
he was burning up
with fever
Momma took off his shirt
put a cold cloth
on his chest
his head
I stood with Silas
next to the wagon
Mr. Casey said we'd all camp
just up ahead
feed the animals
rest
while Momma took a look at Elijah
He was sleeping now
and Momma was praying

Lettie
Nebraska / October 1879

We stayed until the sun set
Didn't no one feel right
I could tell moving on
knowing Elijah was feeling
so poorly
Miss Pratt
pulled together some supper
while Momma
stayed in the wagon
tending to Elijah
Silas was quiet
staring at the fire
Even Sutter
stayed still tonight

not sniffing around
making sure no animals
were in sight
But later after supper
and tents were up
Miss Pratt said good night
to Beau
then took Silas into her tent
Mr. Casey, Mr. Baker, Mr. Spruill came over
to talk to Momma
And I walked quiet
and I bent low
in a corner of dark
under the wagon
to listen
while Sutter slept by the fire

Now we got some choices to make here Sylvia
Mr. Casey
told Momma

Dottie seen to my boy . . .
She can't figure what it is
Momma told him
Her voice was shaky

Problem we have is
Mr. Spruill said
We can't risk it spreading
We seen whole companies wiped out . . .

From cholera
Mr. Baker said

Yes, but Dottie said she didn't think—

Now Dottie's had some nurse training
but she don't know—

Can we just wait one more day?
Momma asked
sounded like just shy
of begging
It was quiet
and then

We talked about it
Mr. Casey said
We can wait a day Sylvia
but then
we gonna have to move . . .
I got the whole company
to think about
you understand
We can't risk the weather
it's getting colder every day
And the truth of it is
I'm worried about everyone else getting sick
We got to stay clear
Can't see no other way

Mr. Spruill said
You know Clara going to make this a long ride
for me
if I leave you behind
Everyone laughed a little
at that

Well . . .
I appreciate y'all waiting
as long as you are
Pray with me
Momma asked
and they did
so long
my legs starting cramping
while I was bent listening
under the wagon
When they went back
to their wagons
I sat and thought
long and hard
about Elijah
about the one day
we had
for him to get better
about what Mr. Casey said
about Elijah's sickness
Spreading
and staying clear
Lest everyone get sick

and all I could think about
was Momma tending to him
And how I was rubbing his back
and Agnes let Elijah drink
from their dipper
and when Silas fell down
and hurt himself
it was Elijah
who spit on Silas's hands

Lettie
Nebraska / October 1879

Funny
I never saw before
how everyone
was getting smaller
and smaller
from all the walking
miles every day
and the days
when we had
just a little bit of food
we had to stretch
and pretend
we weren't hungry
when we were still
wanting more
The few dresses
Momma put in the chest
for me
hung on me loose
where they used to be
tight
and I was taller now
for sure
than when I left home
because my head
was coming up
on Momma's shoulder
where it wasn't before
But Momma's face
was round

her belly too
Agnes saw it first
and then
I couldn't stop seeing it
When is your momma
having the baby?
Agnes asked me
the day before Elijah took sick

My momma?
I asked her
laughing
Why'd you ask that?
Just as I looked
Momma's hand was resting
on top of her stomach
the way I seen my aunt Olivia
do when she was having
my cousin Vivvy

When I didn't answer
Agnes looked at my face
Lettie?
You didn't know did you?

I . . .
She put her hand over her mouth
You didn't know?

I just thought . . .

She's months along already
Agnes said

How do you know so much about babies?
I asked her
not sure if I was more mad
or shamed

I am older than you
and I once helped my momma deliver
she said

A baby?

Yes a baby
I didn't do much but stand there
And it wasn't much different
from the cows
having calves in the barn in spring
Except there was screaming
and my momma was holding our neighbor's legs and—

Well I never seen a cow
having her calf
I didn't want to hear
Agnes talking anymore
about screaming
and holding legs
Lord knows
what was coming next

Agnes laughed
Well you ain't missing all that much
But I do wonder . . .

Wonder what?
I asked her

Why everybody knows
your momma is having a baby
but you

Lettie
Nebraska / October 1879

We sat alone
all day
waiting
for the day to end
for Elijah
to get better
to continue on
The other wagons
stayed away
farther up the road
far enough
so I could just barely smell

the smoke of their fires
and hear some of their talk
Momma stayed in the wagon
with Elijah
praying
keeping him cool
with cloths
giving him castor oil
and making him camphor tea
like she used to
for Mrs. Boston
and that didn't do no good
but I guess
it made Mrs. Boston's family
and my momma
feel better
to be doing something
over sitting by
doing nothing
The way I felt
watching Daddy
in that river
and not being able
to swim fast enough
to save him

Silas
didn't know what to do
with hisself without Elijah

He tried
drawing pictures
in a patch of dirt
with a stick
catching grasshoppers
and butterflies
He even tried getting Sutter
to chase after him
but Sutter
being a good judge
of character
and all
knew Silas
never paid him

no mind any other day
so he couldn't be bothered
with Silas today
There are days
when I think dogs
are just as smart
as mules

I saw Silas
walk out a ways
and sit himself in the grass
staring up at the clouds
I went over
sat next to him
stared up at the clouds too

I miss Presley and Duke
he said still staring up
They always
thought of something fun to do
he said

Like leaving you behind
and throwing rocks
at Sutter?

Well
not that
but other things
He finally looked down
from the clouds
at me
Is Elijah going to die
like Daddy?

Course not Silas
he's just sick is all
I told him
rubbing his leg

Sometimes
Elijah cries at night
'cause he's sad about Daddy
I am too
he told me

We're all sad about Daddy Silas

Elijah says Daddy's in heaven
I nodded
Is he?
In heaven?

Yes Silas
Daddy's in heaven

With Mr. Portee?

Yes

And Mr. Anderson?
he asked
I hope Mr. Anderson
went to heaven too

Mr. Anderson didn't die
he just got hurt remember?

Presley said his daddy said
he died
back in that town
'cause he didn't know how to shoot
his own gun
That's what Presley
told me and Elijah
Silas said

After talking to Agnes
about Momma
and the baby
I had to wonder
If this was something else
everyone in the wagon company knew
but me

Do you miss him?
he asked me

No Silas
I don't miss Presley
or his brother neither

I mean Daddy
Daddy told me I was his baby boy

You were Silas
You were his special baby boy
He nodded his head at me
and his eyes filled with water
And I was his baby girl
I told him
and I miss him
something awful too

Silas wiped his eyes dry
with the back of his hand
and went back
to looking up
at the clouds
I waited as long as I could
then sent Silas
to go hunting for sticks
for the fire we needed to get started

Not far
I told him
not wanting him to get lost
like before
because now
wouldn't no one go looking

It's like we're lepers
Miss Pratt said
stirring cornmeal for the corn cakes
she was getting ready to put in the skillet
She was mad
all day
not at me
I suppose
or Elijah
but at not seeing Beau

You missing Beau?
I asked her finally

Now Lettie
I am worried
about your brother
and worried about
losing too much time
It doesn't make any sense
to me
why we can't keep on
Mrs. Boston traveled ill
the entire way
as I understand it

They think Elijah
has cholera
I said

Pfffttt
I've seen cholera
Miss Pratt said
all over Independence
in fact
And that's not what he has
It's a simple case
of Rocky Mountain fever

Rocky Mountain fever?
I asked her

Yes
she said sure
Fever
diarrhea and such
These men
are making more of this
than there needs to be

That's what Momma thinks
and Miss Dottie too
I told her

Miss Pratt nodded
But men
just have to know more
after all

they are the
authorities
on all
Miss Pratt
just about screamed
the word
authorities

Even Beau?
I asked her

Sit down Lettie
she said to me
We sat
side by side on our bedrolls
I kept on feeding the fire
from where I sat
getting it big
and hot enough for cooking

Yes
it's true
I like Beau very much
she said
But once I get to Nebraska
I have a job
I intend on starting
and a life
I plan on living
alone
But . . .
With Momma inside the wagon
and Silas out
fetching sticks
I could ask
all the questions I wanted
without worrying
about Momma
fussing at me about my manners
But Miss Pratt held up her hand
She's going to make
a very good teacher
I thought to myself
She sure was bossy
as one

A woman has a right
to make up her own mind about things Lettie
and the way I see it
men
shouldn't put a stop
to that

Lettie
Nebraska / October 1879

Agnes's mother came near our wagon
and laid down a kettle
filled to brimming with stew
She waved me over
to come on and get it
There was a cloth underneath
to keep it from scalding
Silas ran over with me
and Mrs. Day backed away as she smiled
at me and Silas

Y'all watch out for your momma and brother now
she said
And eat up that stew
It'll keep you strong

Agnes's momma was kind
I think
But had a way about her
Always sounded like she was bossing
even when she was talking nice

My my my
Momma said later
after we scraped our bowls clean
That Anne
always could put together a good meal

Mmm hmmm Silas said
wiping his mouth with his shirtsleeve

Best squirrel stew
I ever had

Squirrel stew?
Silas looked down at his empty bowl

Silas was particular about what he ate
even out here
on the trail
Miss Pratt got up
to gather our bowls
I was wishing we had more
of Mrs. Day's stew
seasoned up so nice
with berries
and spices Mrs. Day brought with her
and what she gathered
along the way to add
made me feel like we'd never left
after supper
and Miss Pratt and Silas
went to their tents
I went into the wagon
and saw Momma's head
laying on Elijah's chest
They were both
asleep
I took a blanket
and covered them
and when I stepped down
and back outside
Mr. Cole
was there
standing beside the wagon
Mr. Cole?
You're not supposed to—

I do as I see fit Lettie
Came to check in on y'all
See how you're getting on

I told him
Elijah seems the same
So I guess
you'll be moving on
without us

Don't you worry about that
he said
patting my hand
They came on quick
the tears
I guess I'd been holding back all day
Scared about Elijah
and being left behind
They ran down my face
Mr. Cole pulled me to him
and held me tight
and let me cry into his shirt
It was worn
and soft as my daddy's
He walked me to the fire
and sat me down
not letting me go
When the tears slowed
Mr. Cole said to me

I ever tell you
you put me in mind
of my daughter
Malinda?

Mr. Cole didn't tell me that
but Momma said as much
It ain't often
your momma's wrong
about things
Daddy told me once
Just like Sutter
I thought

Malinda got
I say
twenty or so years
on you
but you just as pretty
smart too
He laughed

I smiled with him
Where is she?
Where is Malinda now?
I asked Mr. Cole

Oh
she moved North
some time ago
Once the war ended
she didn't want nothing more
to do with Mississippi
Folks started heading North
and she heard about a school
up there
in New York
Said she had a chance
to get an education
Something me and her momma Polly
God rest her soul
never had
Smart as our girl was
we wasn't going to stop her
Told her to go on
make us proud
and she did just that
Me
I need the land
the air
animals
Not a city
filled with people
Malinda writes
got all her letters in my wagon
Reverend's wife would come over
read them to us

out on the porch
as soon as they came
I don't know who was prouder
of all our girl done
me or her momma
Got her education
working a job where she never

gonna have to answer
to the weather
or the land
like we do
That's what she wanted
and that's what she got
When Polly died
last spring
she came home
I told her then
me and her uncle Oscar
thinking about starting fresh ourselves
out West
She told me
Mr. Cole stopped and laughed
Daddy
it's about time
you got out of Mississippi
She told me
there's a whole country
out there waiting
with opportunity
Mr. Cole spread his hands
wide
Like Daddy used to
He said *opportunity*
like opportunity
was another word
for Nebraska
for West

Do you think
she's going to come visit
in Nebraska?
I asked

Oh one day
I imagine
Hope it ain't
to put me in the dirt
I'd sure love for you
to meet her
One thing my girl showed me

we all got to follow
what we love
don't we Lettie?

That's what my daddy said
I told him

Well then
I'd say your daddy
was a right smart man

Sylvia
Nebraska / October 1879

Sunday mornings stretched long
when you sat
in the pews at Mount Canaan Baptist Church
Benton
Reverend Byrd to everyone else
didn't let the sun
or a timepiece
tell him when he needed to stop talking
God leads
I follow
Benton told the congregation

God don't never tell him
folks got to go home and eat?
Thomas would whisper
too loud in my ear nearly every week
coughing loud
to cover his laughing
I didn't need to feel the eyes
in back of us
see the necks stiffen
in front of us
to know what folks were thinking
but were too kind to say
about my Thomas
When I had to tell my brothers
we were moving
West

to Nebraska
It was Benton
Who said out loud
what most
had been kind enough
to keep to themselves

So when I opened my eyes
to the morning sun
my head still laid across
Elijah's chest
I knew right then
what God had done
and what Thomas
never believed
His skin was cool
to the touch
Elijah's eyes were open
bright
looking at me

Momma?
he said
I'm hungry

Philomena
Nebraska / October 1879

Lettie asked to sit up with me today
as we rode
We weren't expecting
to be moving out
with the rest of the company
but when the day started
and I saw Sylvia
and Elijah
come out of the wagon
both smiling big
looking for breakfast
I had to smile right along with them
We were right after all
I said to Sylvia

Wasn't us that was right Philomena
But God
I asked
and he answered
Sylvia told me

Silas!
I yelled
Someone wants to see you

Lettie went on to tell the company
Elijah was well
Heloise and Ellen Boston
were the first to run over
shouting
God is good and
See what he can do

Elijah didn't want to hear all that fuss
He was steady eating with one hand
while Silas
was hanging on the other

Guess we can move on out
Mr. Casey said

Beau headed straight my way
Glad we don't have to leave you behind
he said

Not today anyhow
I told him
Beau raised his eyebrows at me
Miss Sylvia and Miss Clara
walked behind the wagon
with Elijah and Silas
following behind them
I heard Miss Sylvia fussing
Now you just take it easy
'lijah
and Silas
don't you go messing
with your brother today
I could see

they were hardly listening
already pushing
and shoving

As I told Charly and Titus
to pick it up
the sounds of talking behind us
got quieter
Lettie turned
to look in back of her
Sutter sat between us
his crooked ears
pointed high
Lettie had tied
One of her daddy's
red handkerchiefs
around his neck
I'm not sure
how Sylvia was feeling about it
but Sutter
looked as if he was feeling
more handsome wearing it
and just maybe he was

How are you today Sutter?
I asked him

He stared straight ahead
not paying me any mind

Before I'd left Independence
I'd heard stories
about how traveling West
changes folks
that once you become
a pioneer
you never quite see the country
the same way again
the air
the trees
the sky
all are like new
Because you are
Reborn

Baptized
they say
in the beauty of the land
I could see that now
Back home
I sometimes took the wagon
with Uncle Edmund back and forth
to town
and never once
did I give any thought
to the goings-on
of every day
I never even knew
the names of our horses
But here
traveling through
Missouri
Kansas
and now
Nebraska
I noticed the time of day
just by the shifting
of the sun
and clouds
the sweet scent of sagebrush
after a rain
And I'd grown quite fond
of Charly and Titus
counting on them
as I would dear friends
worrying if we traveled
too long in the day
without rest
or if it was too cold at night
if Titus was eating less
if Charly hadn't been properly
rubbed down
and now
with Sutter by my side
Was I asking a dog
about his day?

Miss Pratt?
Lettie asked
You were laughing

to yourself
she said

Was I?
Just thinking of something funny
I told her

Can I ask you something?

Is this about Beau?
I asked her
knowing already it would be

Well . . . no
she said
It's about my momma

Miss Sylvia?
What is it?

Is my momma having a baby?
she asked
If I hadn't been holding tight
to the reins
I might have fallen off

Lettie
I make it a point
never to meddle
in anyone else's
family affairs
I told her

Lettie stayed quiet
her hand on top
of Sutter's head
holding it there

You been with us
since we left Independence
she said

Yes I have

And when those men attacked our camp

it was you
who held
my brothers
keeping them safe
under the blanket

Yes I did

And then . . .
I could see Lettie
was starting to cry
Sutter looked up at her now too
When my daddy—

Lettie . . .
I said

When my daddy died
in the river
and I couldn't save him
You . . .
You . . .
stood with the men
and dug his grave
even though
they didn't want you to
You learned to drive
Charly and Titus
so we could get to Nebraska
and caught rabbits
for our stew pot
so we could eat

Yes Lettie but what does—

Doesn't that kind of
make you family?

I thought
of all those years
with my aunt Perlie
and uncle Edmund
I was their family
kin

but I felt like
nothing more than
charity

You're right Lettie
Those are all the things
family does for each other

So?

So what?
I asked her

Is my momma having a baby?
I sighed long
Slowed down Charly and Titus
until I could hear Sylvia and Clara
Elijah and Silas

Yes Lettie
Your momma is having a baby

Lettie
Nebraska / October 1879

I could hardly remember
the day Elijah
was born
But I remember
sitting with my daddy
on the porch
waiting
to see my momma
inside
It seemed all day
I had to wait
while Miss Hawkins
from down the road
and Aunt Olivia
came
and sat with Momma
in bed

You just set here with me a bit
Daddy told me
rocking me on his lap
and when it seemed like
all day had passed
he brought me inside
to Momma's bed
and she was holding
a baby
Elijah
Two years later
Daddy did the same
for me and Elijah
when Silas was born
but Silas was screaming
and Momma was so tired
she could barely
keep her eyes open
This one gave her a time
Miss Hawkins said
He'll likely
be a handful

I don't put no stock
in all that
Daddy told her
scooping up Silas
and he quieted right down

Don't go kissing that boy
on the mouth now
lest you want colic
Miss Hawkins yelled at Daddy
and my daddy kissed
Silas again

Two boys
he said to Momma
and one girl
beautiful
as her momma
he said looking down
at me
I remember Momma's eyes

were closed
But her lips were moving
and making the words
Thank you
Thank you sweet Jesus

Sylvia
Nebraska / October 1879

Elijah may have been healed
but he was tired still
I was thankful
after a long day
of trying to make up the miles
we missed
he didn't make a fuss
out of the walking
But I knew he was tired
because instead of racing
and playing with Silas
he walked
along quiet
behind me
while Silas talked
a mile a minute
picking up beetles
and grasshoppers
and any other creature
that was moving
Elijah would say

Mmmhhh
or *looky there*

but that was about all
he could muster

We were too tired
to eat
but I made the children
take bits of jerky
and drink water
so when the boys

235

fell fast asleep
soon as they got out of their clothes
and I started undressing
and saw Lettie
at the flap of my tent
I told her
Lettie baby
your momma's
'bout to fall over
if I don't get some sleep
What you need?

I need to ask you something
she said
Something in her face
told me it couldn't wait
till the morning
and all my tiredness
went away
I stepped out of the tent

Lettie had been riding all day
with Philomena
but her face looked as tired
as I felt
She'd grown so tall
in all the miles we traveled
and prettier
than I ever thought she'd be
I could see her as a woman
smart
strong
just like Thomas always said she was
His Lettie
Letitia
named for his sister
sold away like the others
the one who held him
he said
curled up with him
after their momma was sold
She was the last one
he told me
the last one they took from me

What is it Lettie?

Momma . . .
Are you having a baby?

I reached out my hand
touched her face
so warm
soft
I nodded
and pulled her in to me

Yes I am Lettie
I knew my Lettie
was filled with questions

In my neck
she asked

Why didn't you tell me?
When is the baby coming?
And then
Did Daddy know?
I stepped back
The fire was low
but I could still see her eyes
wide
needing to know

Every day
there was so much
to worry about
I told her
I didn't want
to add one more worry

But did Daddy—

Yes Lettie
Your daddy knew
He was excited
about a baby being born
out West
on new land
free from Mississippi

and the place
that took everything
that mattered
from him

Lettie smiled up at me
Are you?

Am I what Lettie?

Happy about the baby?
she asked me

Well
I told her
I am tired
and most days my back hurts
my feet are already
so swolled
there are times
it hurts to walk
But
I decided
if it's a boy
I'm going to name him
Thomas
Thomas West Grier

Philomena
Nebraska / October 1879

After I watered
Charly and Titus
by the creek
at our midday stop
I could see Beau was waiting
I left our wagon
with the others
and while they grazed the grass
I made my way over to Beau
His hat
shielded his eyes
but I could see his mouth

lips still
full

Thought you forgot about me
he said smiling his smile
I remembered Miss Sylvia's words
Open

How could I forget
about you?
I smiled back

Well
that's what I was meaning
to ask on
He stood
laid down a blanket he was holding
and spread it out for me
I sat down next to him

Hungry?
he asked

You been meaning to ask if I'm hungry?
I laughed

What I'm about to ask
I don't want to do
on an empty stomach
I was hungry
but seeing Beau's face
the manner of his voice
and questioning
made me lose my appetite

No
I told him
I'm not hungry
What is it Beau?

Philomena . . .
He coughed into his hand

Can I get you some water?
I asked

No I'm fine

He kept on
I think you know
I've grown fond of you
I nodded
You're smart
and you speak your mind
and I know
a lot of men
might have a hard time
with your kind of woman

Am I supposed to say thank you?
I asked him

That there is what I'm talking about
Beau said
I thought . . .
I thought you were fond of me too
Beau looked in my eyes
And as hard as I was trying
to listen
my ears started pounding
Philomena?
he asked me

I am fond of you Beau

Then why did it sound like
you were saying
when we left today
you were ready
to leave me behind?
Sounded like
you wasn't feeling
the same way I was

Most of my life
I lived with my aunt Perlie

and uncle Edmund
Even my sister
felt like a stranger to me
right up until she passed
And yet and still
Cold
is what I heard
my aunt Perlie
whisper
to her church friends
about me
Because she lost her natural parents
She ain't like you and me
She had no problem saying
to anyone who'd listen
She is odd
And *she ain't never gonna find a husband*
with her quick tongue
they answered back
And I believed it
I told myself it was why
I had a hard time
with the other girls at my school
and why maybe
I didn't feel the affection
I should with my own aunt and uncle
But out here
on the trail
didn't no one seem to mind
But something now
about Miss Sylvia and Lettie
Elijah and Silas
but especially
about Beau
his kindness
and patience
the way he still admired me
Despite
maybe even because of
the bite of my tongue
looking at me now
the way he was

Philomena
he whispered
Are you crying?

I don't want to be
I said
having a hard time finding my words—

Be what?
he asked

I have to be . . .

Be what?
he said again

My own woman

Beau laughed
so loud
folks stopped eating
and looked over at us
He stopped long enough
to ask

Do you find that
so amusing?
I asked him

You think being with me
means you can't be
who you are?
You smart enough to know Philomena
that who you are
is why I want to be with you
He reached out
for my hand

I reached back
and took his

Sylvia
Nebraska / October 1879

All that stood
between us
and our new home
was wind
our very first snow
and a river
called the Platte

We all slept together
in the wagon last night
tucked in tight
against the cold

Momma
Lettie yelled to me
over the wind
We can't leave him out there
she said
pointing down at Sutter
waiting outside
Thomas's red scarf around his neck
I hadn't noticed earlier
flapping in the wind
We're all he's got
She was wiping
the water from her eyes
Lord knows
it was that Sutter
that done seen her through
the worst of it
I heard her at night
reading to him
saw her during the day
holding him
in her arms
filling the space
Thomas left behind
Elijah and Silas
got each other
and now it seems
Philomena got Beau

I have this baby
and everyone here
in this wagon
counting on me still
to see them through

Get on in here Sutter
I yelled
before this wind blows you away
We were so used to
each other's stink
we slept just fine
warm enough
under all our blankets
with the wind
rocking our wagon
like a cradle

When my body woke
as it does
right before the sun
I remembered again
about the river
and before we got ourselves ready
I pulled them all in close
We bowed our heads
and held hands
in prayer

Heavenly father
we ask you to grant us
safe passage today
as we journey . . .

Over plates
of cold biscuits
Silas shouted

Momma
I'm eating snow
for breakfast
holding out his tongue

Then can I eat
your biscuits?

Elijah said to him
trying to grab away
the food from his plate
that started those two
to wrestling

We don't have time for that now
I told them
trying to keep the scaredness
from my voice

Miss Sylvia
Philomena leaned over
whispered
her hand on my knee
It's going to be just fine
Beau is taking the wagon over
Lettie is going to stay with you
and I'm going to stay with the boys

Both of them?
I asked her

It's very shallow
much shallower
and narrower than—
It will be fine

We'd crossed rivers
since the Kansas
each time
feeling just the same
as the first
seeing Thomas
on that riverbank
the life gone from him
and each time
wondering if it would be me
laid out
my babies standing over me
on a riverbank
but it never was
I made it across every time
to see another day
walk another mile

This would likely be our last
crossing
before our journey ended
There was so much
I'd need to figure out
but somehow
some way
I'd have to find a way
to get to the other side
just like crossing this river

Elijah, Silas
Lettie
Sutter
Time to go

Lettie
Nebraska / October 1879

Mr. Cole
walked with me
on our way to the river
He told me
he and the other men
would get everyone
lined up to cross

Why do women
and children
have to cross first?
I asked him

Well
we got to make sure
we taking care of
the most delicate
in our flock

What does that mean?
I asked him
Delicate?

The ones that need most taking care of
he told me

The ones most likely
to get hurt
I thought then
about when Daddy told me
That's why women
have husbands Lettie
to provide for them
keep them safe
But Momma and Miss Pratt
had come all this way
after we lost Daddy
and we were missing him bad
It was hard
but we were working together
providing for ourselves
safe

Well
I need to make sure
I get Sutter across
Because he needs taking care of
I told him
That's my job

Mr. Cole looked down at me
shook his head
It ain't your job
to save nobody Lettie
You been doing a good job
looking after Sutter
couldn't no one have done better
You loved him
when no one else would
Tom surely would have appreciated that
But there's a difference
between loving
and saving
You a child
and it ain't your job
to save nobody
You get yourself across
walk over with your momma
I'll take care of Sutter
I knew that Mr. Cole
was talking about more than Sutter

He was talking
about my daddy too
and telling me
that maybe my only job
was to love my daddy
as hard as I could
and I sure did that

Mr. Cole?

Yes Lettie?

You said the women and children
were the most delicate
and needed taking care of
because they're the ones
most likely to get hurt?

That's just what I said
He nodded at me

Was Mr. Portee delicate?
or Mr. Anderson
when he shot himself?

Now Lettie—

Mrs. Boston was sick
and she passed I know
But do you think
my daddy was delicate
because he drowned?

Mr. Cole was quiet
and we kept up our walking
I told you once
you put me in mind
of my Malinda
smart as a whip
don't miss a thing
he said to me
Maybe Lettie you right
Sure wasn't the case for my Polly
She worked right alongside me

farming
up until the day she died
She could pick nearly as much
as I could
cook
clean
had our Malinda
and was right back
doing it again
next to me
Maybe delicate
ain't what women are at all
And no
you ain't delicate
just because you get hurt
or die
That was just my way of saying
sometimes men
need to feel
like they got a job
bigger than everybody else's
and looking out for folks
maybe who don't need looking out for

is how men get to feeling
important I suppose
Lettie he told me
laughing now
Why don't you let us men
go on ahead first
and cross that river
ahead of y'all women?

Lettie
Nebraska / October 1879

Even though
Mr. Cole said maybe the men
should cross first
he must not have told the others
because it was still me and Momma
who were the first ones in line
with all the other

women and children
behind us
I knew Momma was scared
so I hurried her
talking all the way
so she wouldn't
look down
We climbed up onto the land
and waited
for the others to cross
Momma bunched up our dresses
behind us
and we sat in the driest spot
we could find

It was almost like
Momma could tell
what I was thinking
because before I said one word
she said to me
Clara told me
we could follow her family
to North Platte
She has people there
William's brother is a barber
and says it's a nice town
for coloreds
Just as nice as Kearney

I couldn't tell if Momma
was asking
or telling

Mr. Cole showed me
on the map
I told Momma
Because that's where he and his brother
Miss Pratt
and most everyone else
are going too
Momma kept on
I know your daddy said
he was aiming to settle in Kearney
but that was before—

we come all this way
and made it through
all we did
We need each other Lettie
Hardest thing
I ever had to do
was leave behind
every one of my brothers
and my sister
back in Mississippi
I thought I was losing
the only family I'd ever have
But these folks here
been family too

North Platte
is just a little bit farther
and I'm sure
Miss Philomena
Miss Clara
Miss Dottie
and surely Mr. Cole
and everybody else
Momma laughed
Wouldn't mind us staying on
With the company
like we been doing?
I nodded
laughing now too

How long we been traveling Lettie?

Five months, four days Momma
I said

Feels like it
We smiled together
And that was before
all I could think about
was what I was leaving behind
It wasn't much
but Lord I miss our home
don't you?
I nodded

but not saying
I was forgetting what it even looked like now
the land where
I was born
where my ma and daddy raised
us up
I thought I wouldn't know
who I was
if I left all that behind
for some place out West I didn't know
And after we lost your daddy
I thought then and there
It was my chance
to turn around
and go back
But something told me to keep going
Now first I thought it was God
Then I was sure it was your daddy
saying
C'mon now Sylvia
you got to follow my dream
But it wasn't neither of those
and both of those
but it was something more too

Something more?
I asked her

It was me
Momma laughed again

But I didn't know that voice
I was following my own mind
for the first time
How about that Lettie?
I was thinking so hard every day
about what I left
about what Thomas wanted
I never once let myself
think about what I found

I was getting mixed up
with Momma's words
The splashing of the water

was getting louder
and I could see Heloise
and Arlene just about at the edge
Agnes was behind them
with her mother
shivering in the cold
everyone else close behind

Momma kept on
Look out there Lettie
All this time
we've been traveling
I've been wishing I was the kind of woman
you could be proud of
Strong like Dottie
Plainspoken like Clara
Smart like Miss Pratt

But you are all those things Momma
I leaned my head on Momma's shoulder
and she put her arm around me

Problem is Lettie
I didn't know it
until now
We made a family
with every one of these folks
So now we got family back home
and we got family here too
and we are gonna be just fine
Ain't we Lettie?

Daddy told me
right before he passed
Not knowing
is the scariest thing there is
I didn't know what
would be waiting for us
when we got to North Platte
but I didn't feel scared

I looked up
and saw Miss Pratt
coming up the riverbank

with Elijah and Silas behind her
laughing and shoving each other
she was holding tight to Sutter
When he saw me
he jumped out of her arms
and ran straight to me
shaking the water from his fur
Yes Momma
We're gonna be just fine

Philomena
Grand Island, Nebraska / October 1879

We said goodbye
to the Bostons
in the town of Grand Island

The Bostons
certainly didn't need
any of us
to escort them
to their new home
where their family was waiting
but I think we all wanted to see
just where they were landing
And after all these months together
give us
just a little more time
before we had to say
goodbye

I'd never heard of the place
before I was told
the Bostons would be settling there
and figured it would be
just a blink
of a town
still growing of course
So I was surprised to see
a town looking so nice
with a railway already laid
and the Platte River running through
Beau told me

that the river
the railway
meant this town
could be one day
be the next Lincoln
and that meant
plenty of work could be found
for Arlene, Helen, Heloise
and their father Merritt

It certainly seemed so
All along the main street
There were pretty white awnings
outside nearly all of the businesses
Bee Hive Grocery
a milling company
a law office
City Hall
one Baptist church
one Catholic

Some of the white folks
stood outside
and watched
as our company traveled past
in a row
I slowed Charly and Titus
when we reached
a small log schoolhouse

In Independence
I thought of little else
but teaching
and a life of my own making
and yet
nearly as soon as my journey began
there had been
the attack on our camp
the loss of Thomas
and learning to drive the wagon
and hunt
and of course
there had been Beau
and thoughts of him

hadn't left room for much else
Now
I realized
I'd have to find some way
to make room for both
I'd barely had time
to think much about my teaching
and my students
and the life that waited for me in North Platte
but seeing this school
I surprised myself
with the fear that rose up in me

Miss Pratt
You feeling all right

I heard Lettie say
from below
walking beside the wagon

Just admiring the schoolhouse
I told her
I clicked the reins
and told Charly and Titus
Get on
We turned down East Second Street
and into the colored section of town
where the Bostons' family were waiting
Charly and Titus
hurried their trotting

Lettie
Grand Island, Nebraska / October 1879

Mr. Boston
always kept to himself
At first I thought
it was because of his sickly wife
and after she passed
I thought he was feeling
the deep sadness
I was
But Momma told me

Mr. Boston
likes to keep his own company
and I could see that
the way he never did much talking
to the men in our company
or even to his own girls
Agnes called him *peculiar*

Something about that man
ain't right
she said to me
when we got to Grand Island
And I don't know how
those girls
are going to ever find a husband
old as they are
and plain too
But I think Agnes
was just saying
what her momma and daddy had

Maybe so
I said back

Even though
I never said much to the Bostons
saying goodbye
was still hard
The Boston sisters
did keep to themselves
except when we sat around the campfire at night
I wondered if they came
to Nebraska
looking for someone to marry
but then I remembered
Miss Pratt
and I thought
maybe they could have a whole life here
in Grand Island
without husbands making decisions
and voting for them

One of the words
Miss Pratt taught me

from an article I read
in the *Independent* newspaper
was *suffrage*
Women who want the right to vote in elections
she said

I thought about how my daddy
wouldn't have liked
hearing about women
making their own choices
about not needing men and husbands
to do their voting for them
Miss Helen, Miss Arlene, and Miss Heloise
sure knew how to work hard
and get along
Even after their momma passed on
I would see them up early
scrubbing clothes in big pots
and making repairs
on their wagon
I think they did more work
than their own daddy
I think they will be just fine
husbands or no
But I didn't say all that to Agnes

Maybe Mr. Boston
was peculiar
and his daughters were quiet
and plain too
but saying goodbye
was still hard

When we got to the home
where they'd be staying
and a man and a woman came running out
hugging them each
hard
Momma stood beside me
Those are Lydia's people
she said
They started around
to the back of the wagon
where Mrs. Boston would have been lying

Mr. Boston put out his hand
stopped them
He started talking to them quiet
His girls behind him
were holding hands
I could see the woman
making just the words

No
No
like she lost her tongue
just now learning
after waiting
all this time for her
that Mrs. Boston
didn't make it to Nebraska
I could feel
the start of tears
and Momma squeezed my hand

They said they gonna come visit
soon as everyone's settled

she said to me soft
turning me to her
so my eyes were on her
and I'd stop my staring
at Mr. Boston
and their family
hurting deep
But my tears kept on

You all right?
Agnes asked
Was it because
we were down now to just six families
from the ten we started with?
Was it seeing the hurt
and thinking all over again
about losing my own daddy?
Or was it after all these months together
I was tired of
having to say goodbye?

Lettie

Nebraska / October 1879

We set up camp
outside of town that night
Sutter rested his head
on his muddy paws
the wind rustled up his fur
while I read from my book

Agnes told me today
that even though her family
is going to North Platte
all they have there
in the way of people
is her daddy's cousin he hasn't seen
since he was a boy
But he told Mr. Day
Nebraska was a good place for coloreds now
He wrote
and told him
every day more coloreds coming
and North Platte
is as good a place as any
to start over
building a future
they can't
in Mississippi
Agnes's momma and daddy
don't want to work the land
like my daddy did
They both
love to cook
were known for it back home
and are hoping
that there
they will finally have the chance
to open a little place
of their own
where they can cook
and people can come
and pay to eat their food
How about that Sutter?

Sutter looked like he didn't have no opinion
on the matter
so I kept on

Agnes asked me to keep quiet
about her momma and daddy's plan
She said they told her and Earl
that sometimes you got to keep quiet
about your dreams
because dreaming out loud
can make other folks
feel like you're thinking too big
So for now
they are keeping quiet
about opening up a place to eat
with pretty white tablecloths
and her daddy cooking in back
her momma serving folks
in front
It's something only family
and now me know
My daddy
would have told Agnes's parents
the only thing wrong about their plan
to open a fancy place in the middle of town
in North Platte
was that
there wasn't no shame
in dreaming
out loud

Philomena
Nebraska / October 1879

It was like crossing
that last big river
and saying goodbye
to the Bostons
made us believe
we were safe
The worst of our traveling
behind us
Up ahead

was the best
of our new lives
just waiting

With just weeks to go
It was foolhardy I know
to let myself believe
that the rest
of our journey
would offer us
its hand in greeting
as if to say
Welcome Home
Not only was it foolhardy
but I have learned
that worse than being a fool
is letting your guard down
so that you're unprepared
for the worst

And because we were
careless
naive
Nebraska slammed the door
in our faces
and reminded us
once again
that just when you think
the hardest part is done
that we you have endured your fair share
the worst
will start up again

When we stopped
midday to rest
Mr. Casey gathered us around his wagon

Looks like a storm is coming in
Hark spotted it there
He pointed high
in those clouds yonder
I could barely see
what he was pointing to
but every one of us

trusted Hark Cole
especially in matters of weather

Looks it like might get bad
Hark spoke up
Let's gather our wagons close
and settle in now
for the day
Get the animals in the middle

Soon as I unbridled Charly and Titus
the wind already started picking up
and I had to pull my shawl over my head
Titus's ears were high
Listening
and he was trotting in place
scared
I rubbed his back firm
saying soft in his ear

You just hold on there
Hold on there Titus
I called out to Lettie
to help me with Charly
But when I didn't see her
I figured
she was trying to round up Silas and Elijah

The first hailstone hit me
square in my forehead
Hard and sharp enough
to break skin
I ran to grab blankets
for Charly and Titus
and covered them as best I could
Sylvia shouted to me
. . .
the . . .
. . .
tie
. . .
rope
But it was so hard to hear now
over the wind coming faster

I had to guess
she was asking me to find rope
to tie down the wagon cover
Tighter
to keep things from blowing away
but I needed first
to lock the wheels in place
and put rocks in front
so the wagon stood still
and store the bridle
and saddles away
The storm was coming so fast
there was no time to talk
just run
and gather
and do
I looked for Beau
and then I saw him
pulling all their oxen
moving slower than ever now
toward the center
with the other animals
You want oxen to move slow
just tell them to hurry
They never do
what you want
when you want
There was still no sign of Lettie
Elijah and Silas
but the clouds
were coming closer and closer

Lettie
Nebraska / October 1879

Mr. Cole told me first
about the storm
but I already knew
because I'd been looking at the sky
and watching all day
the clouds move
like they were dancing
above us

waiting to dump out the rain
they were holding inside
I knew
because Mr. Cole told me
when clouds
hang low
in big dark puffy sacks
a bad storm is coming for sure
Sutter was walking today
along the edge of the road
hunting
for anything that moved
sniffing in the holes
the prairie dogs dug
hoping one would stick his head out
and I was walking with Agnes
After I showed her the dancing clouds
and told her about the storm coming
I looked back for Sutter
but he was gone
Sutter
I shouted
already feeling the wind
blowing from the west
Sutter!
Agnes joined in
and we slowed
looking across the grasses
hoping today of all days
he hadn't gone hunting
He always stayed close
when we walked
out of the way of the mules
and close enough
to watch me
and keep me safe
C'mon now Lettie
Agnes, you come too
Your momma's waiting on you
Momma called to us
Mr. Casey wants us
at his wagon

265

But just as I started over
I saw Sutter
heading off
chasing something
What
I couldn't tell

Agnes pointed and laughed
He's never gonna catch it
she said
But he was going farther from us

Lettie
Momma called again
I looked back to Sutter
getting smaller and smaller
the farther he ran

Tell my momma
I'll be right there
I told Agnes

Lettie, don't—
and before she could stop me
I ran
to Sutter
and into the wind
and the dark clouds
coming closer

Philomena
Nebraska / October 1879

Me and Sylvia
were the last
to get our cover
tied down
I checked one last time
Everything was as tight
as it could be
and I crawled inside after her
closing the flaps
and tying them with the rope
in knots

behind me
Soon as we got inside
and shook out our shawls
we heard

Boo!
Silas and Elijah screamed
jumping from underneath blankets
in the corner

Y'all stay right where you are
Close together now
Till this storm blows through
Sylvia told them
Lettie you too
They looked at her
and at each other

Lettie's not here
they said

This is not the time for games
Sylvia told them
Lettie
she said again
But the blankets in the corner
laid flat
quiet
Sylvia looked at me
I thought she—
I started

Agnes said she was coming right along
Sylvia said
I was so busy getting the boys inside—
We could already hear
the hail beating down
hard on the wagon cover
There was a small tear
in the side
that looked like it would get bigger
if the storm kept up
Sylvia rushed to untie the flaps
I put out my hand

You can't go out
I told her

Lettie's out there

She's most likely with Mr. Cole
Maybe Agnes
Was I asking?
Hoping?
We sat
looking at each other
the boys quiet now
not smiling

Finally I said
I'll go
You stay with the boys

Lettie
Nebraska / October 1879

Sutter!
I screamed over the wind
But Sutter
either couldn't hear
or didn't want to
He had a prairie dog in his sights
and was as close
as he was ever gonna get
The wind was moving faster now
slowing us both down
Sutter!
I yelled louder
He looked back at me
just long enough
that when he did
the prairie dog he was chasing
slipped into a hole
gone
Sutter stopped
looked around and sniffed
His hunt was over
and he came back to me

We got to get back Sutter
There's a storm coming

He looked up
like he just noticed
the weather
and that's when I felt the rocks
coming down on us
at least that's what they felt like
But I could see
they were big round pieces of ice
sharp enough to cut

Run Sutter!
I yelled
But Sutter's mouth was wide open
He was breathing hard
his tongue hanging to one side
He was tired now
too tired to run
after all his chasing

I tried picking him up
carrying him
But I was tripping over
the icy rocks on the ground
So I put him back down
and stood
looking at the camp
so far away now
I could just barely see the white tops
of the wagons
Momma would be mad
worried
most likely both
I put my hands over my head
to stop the ice rocks from hurting
I closed my eyes
not knowing what to do
Sutter barked
but I couldn't look at him now
I wasn't doing my job
taking care of him
I opened my eyes and

269

turned around in a circle
Finally I saw one tree
tiny
off a ways
but closer
than the wagons
C'mon Sutter
I said
running toward it
he followed behind slow
stopping every now and then
to eat the ice rocks
I was just about at the tree
and turned
telling Sutter
to hurry
when I felt myself go down
Deep
into a crack in the field
Deep
into a ditch
like a big prairie dog hole

270

Right before my head hit
I remember seeing Sutter
at the edge
his brown eyes looking down
and the black puffy clouds above me
fading
to nothing at all

Philomena
Nebraska / October 1879

Sylvia pulled out
one of Thomas's jackets
from the chest
His hat too
and I put them on
over my dress and sweater

I wrapped my shawl tight
Don't let her go Momma

Elijah shouted
tears filling his eyes

I'll be just fine
I'm going to see if she's with Agnes
and come right back
I told him

Suppose she ain't there?
Silas asked

Then I'll try the others
We know she hasn't gone far
I'll bring her right back

Promise?
Silas asked

I promise
I told them

I looked at Sylvia
We both knew
I shouldn't be making any promises
I couldn't keep

Lettie
Nebraska / October 1879

My mouth tasted like dirt
and all I could see were eyes
staring down at me
I couldn't count how many
I felt something heavy
on my chest

Lettie?
Lettie?
Sounded like someone calling me
from underwater

Daddy?
I said back

There was a soft rain
coming down now
wetting my face
waking me
from what felt like a long sleep

Let's get her up out of there

We got her now Sutter
good boy

The heaviness on my chest got lighter
and I saw Sutter
being lifted up
and out

Grab hold here—

I heard a man say
Through fuzzy eyes
I saw my daddy
in his hat and coat
looking down at me

Daddy?
I said again smiling
You came back for me

Lettie, it's me Beau
another voice next to Daddy said
Beau Casey
You fell in a ditch
We gonna lift you out now
Just hang on girl

When I was out
they tried standing me up
but my legs wouldn't work
like they should

Just hold on to me
I heard a soft voice beside me

Miss Pratt?

272

Yes Lettie, it's me
Can you see me
One by one
I could see their faces
fuzzy still
but clearer now
Miss Pratt
Beau Casey
Mr. Cole
Sutter stood close

I think she hit her head
Mr. Cole's voice said behind me
I held on to Miss Pratt
and took a step
shaky at first
then another

You can do it Lettie
Charly's right here
she said
pointing in front of me

Help her up Beau
and Beau did
Charly snorted at me
as I rubbed his back
slick with rain
Up high I could see clearer now
the trees
the wagons in our camp
and I remembered running
to the tree
to get away from the ice rocks
and falling
I held on to Miss Pratt
and we rode slow
in the rain
back to camp

Miss Pratt?
I asked
Why are you dressed up
like my daddy?

Sylvia

Nebraska / October 1879

It was too wet to warm Lettie
by a fire
so they brought her into the wagon
I pulled off her wet clothes
rubbed her skin just about raw
with blankets

Momma you're hurting me
Lettie said

You'll want to be sure
her blood is moving
in her arms and legs
Dottie told me
Rub her good and hard
Elijah took one hand
Silas the other
and they rubbed them
till they were bright red
I dressed her warm
and laid blankets on top
Clara brought over warm broth
and Lettie drank it slow
but took it all in
Mr. Cole stood outside

Hark, go on back to your wagon now
I told him
I'll come by later
Let you know how she's doing

But he wouldn't move
I'll stay here just in case
y'all needing something
he told me
Don't mind waiting

Mr. Cole?
We heard Lettie from inside

I'm here Lettie
he shouted back

Can you come inside?
He looked at me
asking

Go on
I told him
and he followed behind
With all of us inside it was tighter
than it'd ever been
but warm too and good for Lettie
She reached out to Mr. Cole
He sat down next to her
and put his big hand on her head

I was wrong about Sutter
he said
You were? Lettie asked

When I told you he got Tom
out of some scrapes
This time he got you out of one too
barking to scare up the devil
till we knew just where you were
Laid down on top of you
keeping you warm
till we could get to you

I watched Lettie nod
tears running down her cheeks
Mr. Cole wiped them away

But why were you wrong?
You said he was good at protecting
she said

Sure did
But I told you too
I think he got nine lives
Turns out
Sutter maybe got ten

Lettie

Nebraska / October 1879

Momma made up a pallet
of quilts in the wagon

I'd feel better
if you slept in here tonight
she said
Stay out of the cold
till your head is better

Momma still didn't know
that the only thing that made me feel better
that could make my head feel better
was being outdoors
and seeing the sky change
from gray
to purple
to black
to gray again
with the moon and stars
above

After she left
I moved my quilt close as I could
to the flap
and opened it wide

All night
I dreamed of Daddy
We were together again
I was sitting close to him
in the wagon and we were back home
having supper
He was talking loud
his mouth full
and I was sitting beside him
in the barn
helping him clean, and rake and polish
in every picture
in my dreams
Daddy was laughing
calling my name

Lettie
Lettie
Lettie
I could feel his hands
on my arms
Lettie
I opened my eyes
to Momma
calling me
shaking me awake
Lettie
It was bright
with the sun shining in
Momma put her hand on my head
You musta had a good dream
because you sure were smiling
she said

I did
not wanting to tell her
about Daddy

How you feeling?

My head hurts
I watched her face
Just a little
I added in
Though it was hurting more than a little
Where's Sutter?

Just outside
We ready to get on our way
But you
gonna stay in the wagon
I nodded
And it hurt to do that

After we ate
we set off
and the bumping made my head
hurt worse than if I walked
When we stopped at midday
I got out to look for Agnes

Lettie!
she screamed running to me
hugging me tight
I was scared
I hugged her back
Didn't I tell you not to go after Sutter?
she said
I nodded
She hugged me tight again
It seemed like such a long time ago
that me and Agnes
couldn't find two words
to say to each other
and now
here we were
hugging each other like we were . . .
not exactly like me and Oda
but a different kind of friends
a kind you can only make on the trail
like this one
who seen
and felt
all the hurts
you been through together
that's the kind of friends
me and Agnes were
I told her
all about getting hit by the icy rocks

That was a hailstorm
she told me
We likely to see more of those
where we're heading

I told her about my hurting head
and Sutter lying on me
and barking
and Miss Pratt
dressing like my daddy
She wrinkled up her face at that
like she smelled something bad
I think Agnes sometimes thought
like some of the men did
that Miss Pratt didn't act the way
a woman should

She was trying to keep warm
I told her
By the time I finished
all my telling
we were ready to start up again

Walk with me
Agnes said holding my hand
My head was hurting less
so I did

Sylvia
Nebraska / October 1879

We passed through
Kearney
Lexington
Gothenburg on our way to North Platte
Tired as we were
we were moving faster than we had
since we left Mississippi
Wouldn't be long
before my new life
would begin

By the time I was not much younger
than Philomena
Sixteen years
God delivered me
from one master
The tiredness of those years
felt more like fifty
Benton preached to us
from his pulpit
from the Book of Exodus
Preached on
Redemption
Salvation
How God delivered
those just like us
slaves
the Israelites
through the miles

across that Red Sea
and out of Egypt
landing here now
Seems more of
God's doing
than man's

As much as I was wishing
Thomas
was here alongside me
and our babies
to make the going easier
what I knew
was that God
not Thomas
would deliver us
once again

Philomena
Entering North Platte, Nebraska / October 1879

I don't know what I was expecting
something small I suppose
enough room to hold a dozen
or so students
Much like the schoolhouse I attended

In my correspondence
I never thought much to ask
and they didn't feel a need
to tell me

Is that the school there?
Lettie asked
Your school?
She and Sutter were sitting up in the wagon
beside me

I guess it is
I said

Should we go inside?
I said to her

We got down
while the other wagons
stopped
in front and behind us

I'll just be a moment
I shouted out

Beau got out
and came over

This it?
he asked me

I shook my head
Yes
He looked the school over
nodding his head
approving
He reached for my hand
and I took it

Inside
it was just as fine a school
as it was outside
In the first classroom
there were windows
looking out onto the street
with rows of desks
and a large one up front
That's yours
Lettie pointed
I walked up and down each row
running my hand
along the desks
I barely noticed the man
who'd stepped inside

May I help you?

Beau breathed in sharp
beside me
and stepped forward

The man was tall
all white
skin
hair
eyebrows even

I'm Philomena Pratt
The new . . .
I started
losing my words

She is the new teacher here
Lettie finished for me

The new teacher?
he asked
He stepped forward
staring

Yes sir
I said
trying to sound
like something I wasn't
Sure?
Proud?

He looked at me hard
I am Mr. Carroll he said

Mr. Carroll?

Yes
He smiled
I am the school director here
in charge of instruction
I believe you have been corresponding
with my colleague
Miss Holmstead
regarding the teaching position
is that correct?

Miss Holmstead
Yes
Yes, of course

I was aware
that I might not
have been making
a strong first impression
I held out my hand
to him
and Mr. Carroll looked down at it
but did not shake it

Welcome to North Platte Miss Pratt
But I expected you
nearly one month ago
he told me

Yes, I do apologize
I wasn't able to secure
rail passage
and traveled overland—
And unfortunately
the company I was traveling with
ran into some unexpected
circumstances . . .

He nodded
quietly
Of course
Of course
he said

I looked around the classroom
and back at Mr. Carroll

Did you know I was . . . ?

Colored?
Here in Nebraska
we do things a little differently
I suspect
than where you're from
he said
We don't have
the resources
for separate schools
and given

all of the . . .
new residents
coming into
our town
Seems we didn't have
any other choice
but to teach
colored and white
together
in our classrooms

I wondered if he could hear
himself
with his
new residents
and
our town
and
our classrooms talk
How long would it take
before coloreds
who moved to North Platte
could count it
as their town too?
He was making his meaning clear
even through
his smile

So I'll be teaching
colored and white students?
Not sure now
this is what I wanted

Is that a problem
Miss Pratt?

I looked at Mr. Carroll
Beau
Lettie
even Sutter
Everyone
looked as if they were waiting
like I had been
felt like
my whole life

to teach
All this way
I traveled to do it
This school
surely wasn't what I expected
but neither were
the last months
of my life

Not a problem
at all
Mr. Carroll
I told him
smiling back

Lettie
North Platte, Nebraska / October 1879

After we left the Bostons
and right before we got to North Platte
I asked Mr. Cole
if he was scared
about starting over again
someplace new
I ain't never spent a whole lot of time
thinking about
whether or not
I was scared
When something's got to be done
I just go on ahead and do it
he told me

What do you think
it's going to be like there?
I asked

I think it's going to be
what we make it

What we make it?
I asked again

First off
we all

your momma too
gonna see our way
to that land office
Choose our plots

And then?

Well then we gonna see what our hard work
gonna get us

That's all?
I said, and stood waiting

Mr. Cole stopped walking
looked down at me
What more was you hoping for Lettie?

It's just that
It sounds the same
as back home
in Mississippi
the hard work
and all

You was thinking
it'd be something different?
Mr. Cole asked me

All these months
when my daddy talked about the West
about all we'd have
once we got here
One thing he never talked about
was the hard work
Daddy made it seem like
everything we wanted
would be waiting on us
All we had to do
was dream
and get here

Do you think we can?

What's that Lettie?
Can we what?
Mr. Cole asked me

Work hard?
Can we work hard
and make it
here in Nebraska?
I asked Mr. Cole

Our folks don't know
how to do nothing else
Lettie
but
work hard

Lettie
North Platte, Nebraska / October 1879

North Platte, Nebraska
was sure a pretty town
Prettier
than the picture
my daddy painted
for me
in the clouds
and bigger too
I couldn't imagine why
you'd ever need to leave
a town
that had everything
Land for miles
all kinds of stores
lining the streets
Agnes's momma and daddy
had surely
found the right
place to open
a place for eating
And just like in
Independence
I saw coloreds
everywhere I looked

Well I'll be
I heard Momma say
as we saw smooth
skinny places to walk
on top of the mud streets
in front of all the shops
so the bottoms of your skirts
didn't have to get caked in mud

Sidewalks?
Momma whispered
to herself
Miss Clara
shouted out
to her husband
There he is William
and it was her husband's brother
a barber in town
standing
out in front of his barbershop
like he'd been waiting
all these months
for just this day
waving his hands over his head
as soon as he saw us
coming through town
We all stopped
and watched them hug and kiss

Silas covered his ears
when we heard
the sound of a train
coming into the station depot
The Union Pacific
Mr. Cole told me
had a depot
in North Platte
and stopped here
going as far West
as Oregon
and California
And for the price of a ticket
rich folks
on that train

288

could sit back
in soft seats
and eat fine food
looking out the windows
at the trails
we had to walk
They don't know
what they missing
Mr. Cole said

I looked down
at Silas and Elijah
walking slow
and pointing
up one street
and down another
And that was when
I saw the office
of the *North Platte Republican*

They have a newspaper here
I said out loud
to myself
but maybe too
to my daddy
wishing again
and hoping
he was watching
from somewhere
all of this
and us too
It was him
after all
who got us here
And I hoped
somehow
he'd know
we made it

Lettie
North Platte, Nebraska / October 1879

Once Miss Pratt
saw the schoolhouse
where she'd be teaching
we all got back in our wagons
and headed over
to the land office
Momma told me to sit in back
with her
while Silas and Elijah
walked beside

What we have left Lettie?
Momma asked

I dug around in the chest
and pulled out
our tin
where we kept our money
Momma watched
her face pinched
as I took out my book
and counted out the money
we had left
what with the supplies
we'd bought
at stops along the way
even with what Miss Pratt
had given
there wasn't much left
I looked up at Momma

*How much do you need
for a plot?*
I asked
Scared now
about the number I wrote down
*I don't think
there's enough here Momma*
thinking
about the food we had
in the wagon

and what we needed to buy
with the cold coming on
and a baby coming too
But Momma dug deeper
in our chest
till she found a small pouch
wrapped in the mixing bowl
that was her momma's
the one
she never let me touch

I kept this aside
from my brothers
and your aunt Olivia
she told me
pulling out the pouch
and counting more coins
in her hand

With your daddy
he would've been able
to get more land
seeing as he had a wife and all
But with just me
I'm only able
to claim half
but should be enough here
for the filing fee
and the claim
But what we get
will be all ours

I added up each one
of the coins
in the book
and showed Momma

That's just enough
for half the acres
Daddy wanted
I told her

That'll have to do
she said

When we got to the land office
I went in with Momma
thinking
This is where my daddy
would have been standing
and I watched my momma
sign her name
thinking
That is where
my daddy
would have signed
and watched my momma
pick out the plot
my daddy would have picked
right along next to
Mr. Casey, Emmanuel, and Beau
Mr. Bruin and Dottie Baker and their baby girl
Mr. William and Miss Clara Spruill and her mother
Miss Lucy
standing tall and proud
when she made her mark
on the paper
the land agent gave her
Agnes and Earl
and their momma and daddy
Agnes squeezed my hand
when I walked past

Mr. Oscar
Mr. Cole
who hugged me to him
hard and close
into his soft shirt
and kissed the top of my head

There's my Lettie
he whispered to me

Miss Pratt said the last thing she wanted
now was a plot of land
to worry about
with a classroom full
of new students to teach
and Beau fussing after her

My hands are full
thank you very much

Mr. Carroll
led us to a tiny little cabin
at the edge of town
when we finished up

As I told you
in my letter
we can't offer much
in the way of compensation
and the accommodations are modest—

This is more than adequate
Miss Pratt told him
And I know she was thinking
what we all were
that after our time
on the trail
in tents
and in back of our wagon
this cabin
would suit us all
just fine
Me and Momma
Silas and Elijah
looked around the log cabin
One small window
sat up high
across from the fireplace
Miss Pratt told us
we could all stay
with her
making room
for us
just the way
Momma made room
for her
when there was none

Just till the baby is born
Momma told me
and we can build

our own home
That means
when the weather warms
and the ground thaws
I know

Thank you Mr. Carroll
Miss Pratt said
when he left out
We held each other tight
and Momma prayed
long and hard
For God's deliverance
and for our safe arrival
for our home
for our family

Lettie
North Platte, Nebraska / November 1879

In back of the cabin
there was a barn
just barely big enough
for one mule
let alone two
but Charly and Titus were warm
squeezed in close together
Just like us
I don't think
they minded one bit
I kissed Charly on his nose
Good night
I told them both
before I fed
and covered them
and closed the door
and headed out to the tent
where Sutter was waiting

From where we sat
we could see the lantern
lighting up the cabin
and imagine

the warmth inside
our new home
in the West
in Nebraska
with a fire in the hearth
and beds stacked with quilts
Silas, Elijah, Momma
and Miss Pratt inside
But me and Sutter
liked it best
curled in close together
warming each other
best as we could
in the tent
Momma let me pitch outdoors

You gonna have to sleep inside soon
Momma said
wrapping me in a shawl tonight

I know Momma
I told her

Outside
in the tent
I pulled the stack
of papers
Miss Pratt gave me
from the schoolhouse
and the pencil sharpened
good
and laid the papers flat
on top of my book
It was nearly filled
with my writing
dirty
and curled around the edges
Some grease
and dirt stains
were on the front cover
and where I had written
Our Trip West
back when we left
Mississippi

months ago
was nearly faded away
to nothing
But tonight
I didn't need the book
I just needed the paper
Miss Pratt gave me
and my new pencil

My fingers were cold
and stiff
but I started in
knowing already what I was going to write

My dearest Oda . . .
Oda is my best friend
back home
I told Sutter
I don't know
If you'll ever get to meet her
but if you do
you'll love her
same as I do
I told him
So I'm going to write
and tell her
all about
everything that happened
and about you too
How we took care of each other
the whole way
I scratched his ears
the way he liked
and he looked at me
listening
so she'll love you
just like I do

There was a bite of cold
outside
in the air
I knew
Momma was right.
that it'd soon be too cold

to sleep outdoors
The snow would pile high
and a shawl wrapped tight
quilts piled on
Sutter curled in tight
and our thin tent
wouldn't do much
to keep away the cold

But for tonight
it was just right
for me and Sutter
me writing
and reading out loud
and us
listening together
to the night sounds
calling out
far away in the night
under one big open sky

. . . .

AUTHOR'S NOTE

The lives of children who have been uprooted from their homes and have to navigate the challenges of leaving everything they know behind to begin again are at the heart of my first middle grade novel, *Finding Langston*, and the two sequels, *Leaving Lymon* and *Being Clem*. These books all center on the period historians describe as The Great Migration, the era when nearly six million Blacks left the South for better opportunities up North. But after those novels were out in the world, I discovered an article about Exodusters, a term used for the exodus of the thousands of Black homesteaders who migrated from the South to the West during the period of Reconstruction. In the article, this mass exodus was described as the *first* Great Migration. I was stunned. The *first* Great Migration? And then . . . *Black pioneers?*

As a child, I grew up with many of the same mythologies about the West that so many others had. Brave pioneers traveling across wide expanses

of scenic prairie land in covered wagons, cooking under the stars over an open fire. And, like many young readers of my generation, I read the Laura Ingalls Wilder Little House on the Prairie series, and was unaware that Laura's family illegally made their home on Osage land. When I read this series, I was oblivious to the negative portrayals of Indigenous populations and the positive depictions of those who made their homes on stolen ancestral lands. Lettie's family began their travels in 1879, decades after President Andrew Jackson's 1830 Indian Removal Act. Unlike earlier pioneers traveling along the Oregon Trail, Lettie's family most likely would not have encountered many Indigenous people. By the late 1800s, millions of Native American people had been lost to multiple Indian Wars, murder, and disease, or relocated to reservations on Indian Territory in Oklahoma, Kansas, Nebraska, and Iowa.

As a young Black girl reading the Little House

on the Prairie stories, I could never quite lose myself in Laura's narrative because the one question that always lingered was, *Where are the Black people?* I love exploring ideas of freedom, especially as it relates to the history of this country. Whether it is stories from the prairie or from northern cities, the question for me remains: *Where do Black people go in this country as they seek out the freedoms that should be afforded all of its citizens?* What Black people hoped would be freedom, first following the Emancipation Proclamation in 1863, then the end of the Civil War in 1865, and then Reconstruction through 1877, never came. Instead, they experienced increasing disenfranchisement, fear, and racial violence. Black Codes were implemented, which outlawed Black ownership of land, Black entrepreneurship, and quality education for all and ushered in the rise of the Ku Klux Klan. Often unable to purchase land, Blacks were forced to remain tenant farmers, sharecroppers to their white landlords, working for low wages, essentially a form of re-enslavement.

But in 1862, the US Congress passed the Homestead Act, which was intended to develop the western portion of the United States. This act offered Black people a chance at long-awaited freedom in the form of land ownership. However, in 1862, when the act was signed into law, Black people, along with Chinese and Native American people, were ineligible to file claims under the Homestead Act, as they were not considered citizens of the United States. For Blacks, citizenship arrived in the year 1868 with the 14th Amendment, which granted citizenship to formerly enslaved people. Native Americans, many of whom saw their ancestral lands stolen and distributed as part of the Homestead Act, were granted US citizenship in 1924. Chinese immigrants finally became US citizens in 1943. The only group able to waive the US citizen requirement were European immigrants. As farmers in their homelands, many immigrants were drawn to the United States and the promise of free land and ample agricultural opportunities. In the 1800s, over five million German immigrants alone settled between Missouri, Ohio, and Wisconsin in what became known as the "German Triangle."

For just a small filing fee, equaling $18 in today's economy, US citizens and European immigrants could claim their own 160-acre parcels of undeveloped land in thirty states. Each claimant was required to improve or "prove up" their land by building a structure and planting on cultivated land within five years or risk forfeiting their claim. But with difficult terrain, unpredictable weather, limited funds to purchase supplies, inadequate knowledge of farming, death, and disease, proving up was more difficult than most expected. Of the four million homestead claims filed, only 1.6 million deeds became official. The most successful claims were located in North Dakota, Colorado, Montana, and Nebraska. Nearly 270 million acres of free land were distributed through 1976 when the law was repealed.

In 1873, a man named Benjamin "Pap" Singleton began visiting Tennessee to recruit Blacks to travel with him to the Promised Lands of Kansas, or "The Negro Canaan," as Kansas was called by many Black emigrants, and claim what was rightfully theirs under the Homestead Act. Singleton, who was born into slavery in 1809, called himself "The Black Moses." He was drawn to Kansas because abolitionist and activist John Brown had based his antislavery crusade there.

Word of the opportunities in the West began to spread throughout Black communities, not all of it accurate, and in 1879, Blacks began boarding steamships arriving in St. Louis, Missouri, with the plan to continue their journey to Kansas and states further west along various trails. The period of 1879–1880 became the year of the largest great migration on record, with 20,000 Black people departing the South for the West in a single year. Their best chance of survival, they felt, was to stay together. So together they traveled in all-Black wagon companies and then settled within colonies of other Black settlers. Some of the largest of these settlements were in Nicodemus, Kansas; Dearfield, Colorado; Sully County, South Dakota; Dewitty, Nebraska; Empire, Wyoming; and Blackdom, New Mexico. In Nebraska alone, nearly 3,500 Black claimants obtained claims from the land office and were granted ownership of nearly 650,000 acres of land. As many as 15,000 Black family members lived on these homesteads.

During my research trip to the Museum of

American Homesteading in Beatrice, Nebraska, and the National Frontier Trails Museum in Independence, Missouri, many of my romantic notions of pioneer travel were put to rest. Covered wagons, often called "prairie schooners," were typically so small and uncomfortable that families rarely sat in them during travel. In addition, on warm days, temperatures under a wagon's canvas cover could rise as high as one hundred and ten degrees Fahrenheit. As a result, passengers were required to walk the grueling hundreds, sometimes thousands, of miles in extreme weather while battling chiggers, fleas, flies, gnats, lice, scorpions, snakes, and wild animals along the way. They would often go weeks without washing. Lighter loads in a wagon also helped to save the strength of the oxen and mule teams pulling the wagons. Mules, a cross between horses and small Mexican donkeys, were the best-suited animals for the long journey west. The most common, the Missouri mule, was stronger than horses and faster than slow-moving oxen, could withstand heat, ate minimal feed, had strong legs and hooves, and because of their good peripheral vision, were surer-footed than horses. Their keen sense of smell meant they could detect dangerous predators from long distances. Mules have often been tagged with the label of "stubborn," but they use their large brains to carefully weigh the threat of danger and "stubbornly" refuse to advance unless they can first be assured that they are safe.

For formerly enslaved Black men, the West ushered in new jobs as Pullman Porters on "Iron Horses," the transcontinental trains that ran from Council Bluffs, Iowa, to Oakland, California. Black men who fought during the Civil War were recruited out West in removal actions against Native peoples. They were nicknamed "Buffalo Soldiers" by Native Americans because their skin color and curly hair were thought to resemble those of buffalos. And finally, the newly freed men who were left behind to care for cattle as slave-owning Texas ranchers fought with Confederate troops were now needed to move herds of cattle to feeding grounds across the plains and were hired as cowboys. Nearly one in four cowboys were Black men, including some more notable names such as Nat Love and William "Bill" Pickett.

But it was reading the primary source materials of women and children that most shattered my misperceptions of the West. Deaths and injuries were especially common in children along the trail who were more likely to fall out of open wagons or have clothing caught in wagon wheels. Nearly ten percent of all homesteaders were women. Unlike married women, divorced, widowed, deserted, or single women were eligible to claim and own land under the Homestead Act as long as they were considered to be the head of a household. On their own, they proved up at nearly the same rate as their male counterparts. Many of these women included Black women homesteaders such as Bertie Brown, a single woman from Missouri who filed a claim while in her twenties, and Annie Morgan, a widow and former cook for General Custer. Both women successfully proved up their claims in Montana. Lucretia Marshbanks, a formerly enslaved woman from Tennessee who in freedom worked as a cook and owned a hotel, successfully homesteaded in Wyoming until her death in 1911.

The diaries of women made particular note of the landscape through which they traveled, the personalities of their travel companions, and the relationships they formed with others in their wagon companies. And unlike the historically inaccurate portrayals of violent encounters with Native Americans, women wrote of the often-friendly encounters they experienced with Native peoples, in particular with women who traded with them and taught them skills like curing meat and fish, foraging, and identification and use of medicinal plants. Indigenous men helped with fording rivers, crossing and navigation, and otherwise ensuring the pioneers' survival. The emotional pain was evident, mainly in the works by women and children who wrote of the difficulty of leaving family and friends and all they knew *behind*. This was in sharp contrast to the accounts of men who tended to outline their hopeful vision for the land, wealth, and independence that lay *ahead* in the West. And yet, babies born in the West were often given the names of landmarks their mothers passed en route to their destinations including *Nevada*, *Gila* (for the Gila River in Arizona), and *Columbia* (after the Columbia River.) In the 1800s, women were most often powerless in making the decision of whether to undertake this long, difficult journey. Nearly one quarter of them were pregnant. A good amount died along the way from accidents, disease, and drownings. After the death of a husband or father, they were expected to carry on alone. Many pioneer families traveled with their dogs and cats too. They were invaluable companions, but also quite helpful in hunting down dinners of rabbits, gophers, and squirrels.

Whether it is 1879 or 1946, the first Great Migration or the second, the West or the North, freedom has always been sought out by Black people in this country, but especially with the thousands of Black pioneers who left everything behind and set out to start again in the West.

. . . .

ACKNOWLEDGMENTS

I began this book much like the pioneers who began their travels West, unsure and unknowing, but trusting that my journey would land me where I was meant to be. I am eternally grateful for all those along the way who offered their guidance.

My editor, Mary Cash, who is seemingly willing to be my partner on most any writing journey. She is a fearless traveler and guide and I am immensely thankful for her continued support.

Thank you to author friends Traci Sorrell, Heidi Stemple, and Sue Gallion, who demanded that I make my way West for research. I cannot express my gratitude for Sue who opened her home, pulled out a map, and traversed three states, museums, and countless attractions for miles and miles. RIP Tucker—you too were a wonderful host.

Thank you to my cousin Vicky Smith and her suggestion of reading *Flyin' West* by Pearl Cleage, and Nancy Nash who loaned me her copy of *Women of the West* by Cathy Luchetti and Carol Olwell during a visit to Peaks Island, Maine.

Thanks for the wisdom of friends who made the going easier with their expertise and support. Rob Winess, Mike Kristofik, Melanie Hall, Ann. Burg, Virginia Euwer Wolf, Stef Tolan, Fox North, Kelly Braffet, Nancy Castaldo, Alysa Wishingrad, and Julie Chibarro.

And, as always, a very special thank you to the warm and steady guidance of my agent, Rosemary Stimola of Stimola Literary Studio.

I am grateful to all of the people and places that offered me the space to find story in quiet, community, good food, and the beauty of nature: The Highlights Foundation, The Illustration Institute, Candace Fleming, Liz Rusch, and the MacDowell Colony.

Thank you to the knowledgeable staff at Homestead Heritage Center in Beatrice, Nebraska, and Pioneer Trails Adventures and National Frontier Trails Museum in Independence, Missouri.

Thanks to my incredible assistant, Mya Rose Bailey, who makes everything so much easier with her tireless research and problem-solving skills. And my sister-in-law, Darlene Cline, who during her visit to Nebraska returned with materials that helped me to course correct along the Oregon Trail.

Thank you to Dutchess County ASPCA who helped me to foster and then adopt a nine-year-old pitbull rescue named Miles Morales. He brought so much joy to my life when I needed it most. Though his time with me was short, the love he left behind is everlasting. In his story, I found Sutter's.

And finally to my family, James, Jaime, Maya, Malcolm, and Leila. Your unwavering support sees me through each day.

Each book I read helped me to better understand the courage, fear, and sacrifice of the travelers, and I am so thankful to those who left behind their stories allowing each of us to learn and experience some small part of the lives they lived. These are just several of the many I used in my research:

Exodusters: Black Migration to Kansas After Reconstruction by Nell Irvin Painter

The Oregon Trail by Rinker Buck

The Bone and Sinew of the Land: America's Forgotten Black Pioneers and the Struggle for Equality by Anna-Lisa Cox

Black Pioneers: An Untold Story by William L. Katz

Prairie Lotus by Linda Sue Park

The Snow Fell Three Graves Deep: Voices from the Donner Party by Allan Wolf